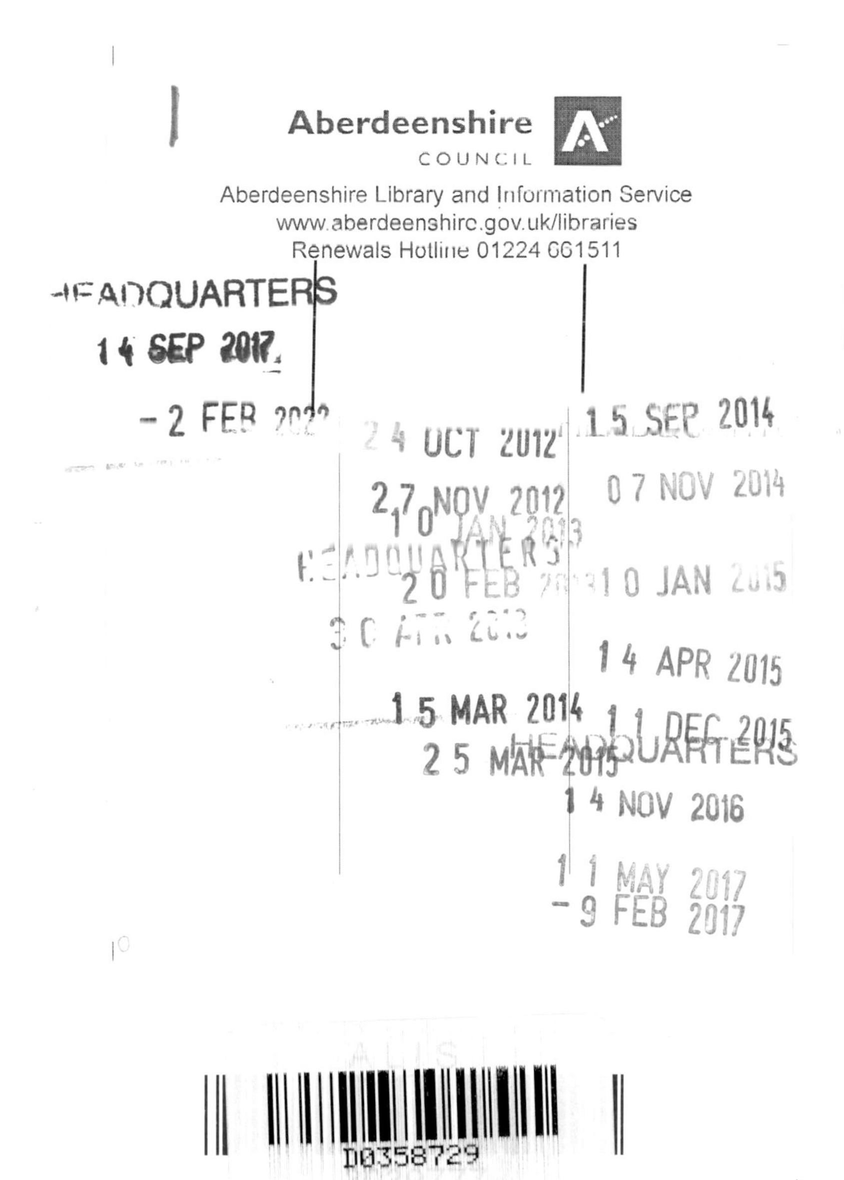

Hope's Last Chance

In a last, desperate bid to save their family farm from repossession, brothers Tom and Jeb Hope head west to California to take a chance on an old mining claim. Against all odds, they find gold . . . but then calamity strikes.

When young Jeb heads for the bank with his precious find, he is robbed and wounded. Then, when he tries to recover the gold, he is murdered in cold blood, leaving his loyal brother Tom devastated.

Now Tom must follow the trail of his brother's killers and find the gold which can save his family. His search takes him from the docklands of Sacramento, through the lawless mining towns of the Sierra Nevada and on to hostile Indian territory where danger is everywhere. Does he have what it takes to survive?

By the same author

Rangeland Justice

Hope's Last Chance

Rob Hill

ROBERT HALE · LONDON

First published in Great Britain 2011

ISBN 978-0-7090-8986-5

Robert Hale Limited
Clerkenwell House
Clerkenwell Green
London EC1R 0HT

www.halebooks.com

For Val and Joss

Typeset by
Derek Doyle & Associates, Shaw Heath
Printed and bound in Great Britain by
CPI Antony Rowe, Chippenham and Eastbourne

1

Three men closed on Jeb. Two stepped out in front of him, handguns drawn. One was heavy-set and had his black hat pulled down low. An older man, flint-eyed and with a ragged beard, was beside him. A younger man appeared behind him, aiming his Colt at Jeb's spine.

The mountain track narrowed here between the two huge boulders which had concealed the men. Jeb dropped the shotgun he had been carrying and raised his hands. The saddle-bags, which had been slung over his shoulder, slipped on to the stony path.

'I ain't got nothin' you want, mister,' Jeb began. 'I was just goin' down to pick up supplies.'

'Shaddup,' the first man snarled.

'Look in the bags, Buck. Do I have to tell you to do everythin'?' the older man said.

The man standing behind Jeb holstered his gun and picked up the saddle-bags.

'Them's empty, Pa. Ain't nothin' in 'em but mountain air. Look in 'em, Heck.'

'I tol' you,' Jeb began again.

'An' I told' you.' Heck smashed the side of his gun into Jeb's face.

Jeb reeled and held up his hands in a vain attempt to protect himself, blood welling from the cuts on his cheek. Heck shoved Jeb backwards and kicked his legs away from under him, sending him sprawling.

The older man laughed. 'See that, Buck? You watch yer brother. Heck knows what he's doin'.'

'Take off yer booots,' Heck commanded, 'and shake 'em out so's we kin see.'

Jeb pulled off his boots one by one, held them by the toes and shook them over the path, so that anything hidden inside would fall out. Nothing did.

'Geddup,' Heck snapped. 'Whatcha got in your pants' pockets?' He glared at his brother. 'Damnit, Buck, search 'im, will ya?'

The man standing behind him hauled Jeb to his feet. He patted down Jeb's pockets and looked in the pocket of his cotton shirt.

Jeb's mouth was too full of blood for him to speak. His cheekbones throbbed from the pistol blow.

'Whyn't we go on up to his claim and look there, Heck?' Buck ventured.

'Ain't you bin listenin', Buck? He's on his way down to buy provisions. These damn miners, they ain't got no money, they pay for everythin' in gold.'

Jeb spat out a mouthful of blood. 'Ain't found no gold. Store gives us credit.'

Buck said, 'Hear that, Pa? That's a barefaced lie. Ain't no store in the whole of California gives credit to miners.'

The older man considered. 'Look in his mouth,' he barked.

Jeb shut his mouth tight.

'Grab 'im, Buck,' the older man said.

Buck seized Jeb's arms from behind. The older man slammed his fist into Jeb's belly, cutting off his wind. Jeb gasped in mouthfuls of air. The older man nodded to Heck who held Jeb's face upward with one hand while peering into his mouth. Just to make sure, he shoved two fingers of his other hand into Jeb's mouth to feel for anything hidden in his cheeks. Jeb clamped his teeth down hard. Heck screamed wildly and tried to shake his hand free. The older man stepped forward and slammed Jeb in the gut again. Heck yanked his hand free. He hopped from foot to foot, whimpering like a whipped dog, trying to shake the pain out of his hand.

'Shaddup, Heck,' Pa said. 'Quit hollerin'. I'm tryin to think.'

'He damn near bit through the bone,' Heck sobbed. 'Damn near bit two o' my fingers off.'

Buck grinned.

'Look in his boots again,' the older man said.

Buck shoved Jeb aside and stuck his hand down into each of Jeb's boots.

'Well, lookee here,' Buck said and pulled out a small leather bag which had been stuffed into the toe of the second boot.

The older man snatched the purse. He undid the lace and tipped out the contents. A small pile of gold nuggets gleamed in the palm of his hand. Buck and his pa laughed out loud. Heck nursed his fingers.

'Damn you, Buck,' Heck moaned. 'If you'd looked there in the first place, I wouldn't have got bit.'

'Sure glad we ran into you this mornin', young fella,' the older man jeered.

Heck picked up Jeb's scattergun with his good hand.

'This ol' thing still work?' He waved it casually in Jeb's direction. 'You keep it loaded?' As he asked, he pulled the triggers and loosed off both barrels. The crash echoed round the mountain. Jeb took most of the shot in his thigh. He screamed with pain and collapsed on the ground. Heck laughed. 'Gonna keep you busy from here till Sunday, pickin' that buckshot out. Come on boys.'

Heck threw the scattergun to the side of the path. It clattered a few yards down the rocky slope. He snatched up the leather saddle-bags and took them with him. Jeb writhed in agony, clutching his thigh. The three men turned and headed down the track to where they had tethered their horses.

Jeb tried to collect his thoughts. No one would have heard the shotgun. Even if they had, they would assume it was someone out hunting rabbits. Anyway, almost all of the claims this high up the mountain had been worked out and abandoned. His own claim, which he worked with his elder brother, Tom, was over a mile up the path. Doc Morgan's cabin was the nearest human habitation.

Jeb's leg was alight with pain. He hauled himself along on his side with his elbow and by shoving with his good leg. He pushed himself off the path and across the slope in the direction of Doc Morgan's place half a mile away. He had to keep stopping to rest. The buckshot burned in his thigh and, heaving himself along like this, he felt the sinews in his shoulder crack.

Doc Morgan had built his cabin by a stand of mountain maples and a stream which danced down through the woods. He had arrived years before the miners and set about collecting botanical specimens, making medicines and building a still. He made contact with the local Paiute

Indians and traded his rot gut whiskey for their herbal remedies. Originally he had intended to spend one year in the Sierras and then make his fortune by selling his own line of medicines on the coast. Somehow he had spent more time with his still than with his remedies. Since the miners arrived in 'forty-nine, he had passed most of his sober hours treating calloused hands and broken bones.

When he could see the cabin, Jeb called out, hoping Doc was there. The place was silent. He hauled himself the remaining yards, almost blacking out with the pain. He pushed open the cabin door and was confronted by the soles of Doc Morgan's boots. Doc had collapsed dead drunk the night before and was asleep where he had fallen. Jeb shook his foot until he heard the doc groan and curse himself into wakefulness. Doc sat up and rubbed his bleary eyes.

'That you, Jeb? Damnit to hell, what've you done to yourself?'

Muttering and cussing, Doc got to his feet and lifted Jeb on to the bed.

Back at the mine, Tom Hope finished the letter he was writing. His dog, a scruffy mongrel named Boss, lay contentedly at his feet. The letter was to Ruth, his sister back in Missouri. She had stayed home to look after their pa while Tom and Jeb came to try their luck in California. Like many small farmers in that region, the Hopes were dirt poor. The threat of bank foreclosure hung over them and their richer neighbours angled to buy them out. After three wet summers and bad harvests, Pa Hope was broke, in poor health and the farm was more than he could manage. But he refused to sell. The farm was all he had.

When news of the discovery of gold in California galloped across the country, twenty-year-old Tom Hope and his younger brother Jeb packed their few belongings, took all the money they could borrow and headed West. The boys were glad to be away from the grinding poverty brought on by poor harvests, and from watching their worried, widowed father decline in front of their eyes. One lucky strike in the goldfields and their problems would be over for ever. They would redeem the mortgages, buy the farm outright and pay for their father to receive the medical attention he needed.

Instead, when Tom and Jeb reached California, they fell prey to all the scams that lay waiting for them. They were overcharged for tools and they were forced to pay ridiculous prices for food. The only mineral claim they could afford was an old shaft which the original forty-niners had worked to death. It was up an inaccessible mountain path, five miles from the nearest settlement, a tiny mining community called White Fir.

No one worked the neighbouring mineshafts. The gold seams were exhausted. The miners had either left to pan for gold on the Feather River or given up and gone home. Only Tom and Jeb were working at this altitude on the mountain now. The Hope boys had dug, shovelled, hauled rocks and crawled on their bellies in the earth every day for a year.

Today they had awarded themselves the day off. Their dreams had come true. Twenty feet below the floor of the original shaft they had discovered a new seam. And yesterday Tom hacked out a handful of nuggets the size of sparrow's eggs.

In order not to attract attention the boys had decided

that Jeb would take the gold to the Wells Fargo bank in Sacramento on his own. Down in White Fir, where he would have to catch the Butterfield stage, people were used to seeing one or other of them buying supplies. The Hopes had a reputation for working hard and if Tom and Jeb were away from the claim together, everyone would know something was up.

In the early days, when White Fir was just a collection of tents, it had been a peaceful place. The miners helped each other out and worked hard at their own claims. Recently, all manner of drifters and rogues had ended up the area, all intent on making a fast buck. Now, with no law enforcement to protect people and with the gold starting to run out all over the Sierras, fights and robberies were common. Everyone had to watch his back.

Tom wrote to Ruth as often as he could. He was homesick. He longed for her letters and danced a jig when they arrived. He was particularly concerned to hear how his father was. The emphysema the old man had contracted as a child, working down the coalmines in his native Sweden, had weakened him. He was getting worse. When Tom and Jeb announced that they were going to California to mine for gold, he forbade them outright. The thought of his sons working underground was too much for him to bear. Then when he saw that the boys were going to go whatever he said, he reluctantly gave them his blessing. He also saw that, if they wanted to keep the farm, gambling on a gold strike was their only option.

Assuming that Jeb had already caught the stage to San Francisco, Tom stuffed his father's old pistol into his belt and started down the mountain to the Pony Express office at White Fir. He got there at noon. The San Francisco stage had left on time, so he assumed Jeb was well on his way by now. The Pony Express clerk took his letter and estimated that it should arrive at their office in Kansas City inside of sixteen days.

Since the Hope boys had arrived a few wooden buildings had sprung up in White Fir, but in the main the settlement was still a collection of tents. Men were eating at trestle-tables in the open air. A woman was serving mutton broth and boiled onions at a dollar a plate. The food smelt like heaven to Tom as he walked past, but he guarded what little money he had. He and Jeb had survived for months on sourdough bread, acorn coffee and any rabbits they could shoot.

There was no saloon. Instead, an Irishman sold bottles of red-eye out of the back of a wagon. He had arranged a few tables and benches close by. A group of men sat drinking and playing cards. Tom crossed to the other side of the street to where the horses were tethered.

Everyone looked up as a freight wagon rolled in loaded with wooden packing-cases and with a piano roped on tight. A fierce-looking woman with flame-red hair and a skinny, fox-faced man were sitting up front with the driver. The woman held a wicker basket containing a ginger tomcat on her lap. As the wagon pulled up, the woman stood up, put down the basket on the seat behind her, and grandly addressed the street. 'This White Fir?' she boomed.

'Sure is, ma'am,' someone called back to her.

'Well, White Fir, y'all got a nice surprise comin'. I'm Dixie Spinette, an' this here's my partner Ruben Sharpe,' she indicated the man sitting beside her, 'but you kin call him Frenchie. We're gonna open a saloon for you boys.

Gonna be the best for miles aroun'.'

'Gonna be the only one for miles aroun',' someone called back.

Dixie wasn't put off. 'That's what I'm sayin',' she continued. 'We gonna have music, singin', dancin' an' proper whiskey. None o' that coffin varnish you boys are used to. We gonna have girls. I know you boys git mighty lonesome up here fer want of a bit o' female company. An' these are nice girls too. I ain't havin' no calico queens work for me.'

The miners watched Dixie open-mouthed.

'We gonna have gamin' tables. Who don' like to play a hand o' faro of an evenin'? Who don' like a game o' chuck-a-luck to pass the time? Frenchie here, he's in charge of the tables.'

The miners mumbled approval to each other.

The man serving red-eye from his wagon was stony faced. 'You sayin' my whiskey ain't no good, lady?' he called.

'Ain't never tried it,' Dixie came back. 'So's I couldn't say. Looks the right colour though.' She laughed. 'I knowed a man once sold some concoction made up of burnt sugar, alcohol an' a spit o' tobacco juice. That was the right colour too.'

'That's what you put in yours, ain't it, Bill?' one of the drinkers joined in.

'No, it damn well ain't,' Bill fumed. 'You've drunk enough of it so you should know.'

'Now, I need some of you gentlemen to help us unload this here wagon,' Dixie announced. 'The sooner she's unloaded, the sooner White Fir kin have its saloon. Come on, now. It's in the interests of the community.'

Tom had been standing on the other side of Dixie's

wagon from the drinkers. Panning equipment was tied on to one of the tethered horses. Beside it, he noticed his own saddle-bags, the ones Jeb had been carrying with him when he left camp that morning. His blood ran cold. Those bags and the pistol he had stuck in his belt had been a present from their pa when they left home. Jeb would never have parted with them willingly. He scanned the drinkers and the men eating at the tables but there were so many new faces among them that he couldn't identify who the horse might belong to. Tom joined in the unloading of Dixie's wagon, never taking his eyes off the saddle-bags.

As Tom was shifting one of the packing-cases, three men got up from the dining table, belching and wiping grease from their moustaches with the backs of their hands. They strolled over towards the horses. One man was older with a ragged beard and a hard, weathered face. The other two were in their twenties, heavier built, but only a few years older than Tom. All wore Navy Colts in their gunbelts. Frenchie asked them for a hand with the unloading as they passed, but they waved him away.

One of the younger men untethered the horse with Tom's saddle-bags on it.

'Hey, mister,' Tom approached him. 'Them's my saddle-bags. I kin prove it.'

The man looked anxiously about him. 'You're mistaken, fella. They ain't yours. Now git.'

'They've got my pappy's name writ on the inside,' Tom said. 'My brother was carryin' 'em when he left camp this mornin'. Now how come you've got 'em? An' where's Jeb?'

'I told you,' the man lowered his voice. People were

beginning to look in their direction. 'I tol' you to git. Now you move outa my way.'

'What's the trouble, Heck?' The older man walked towards them, eyeing Tom coldly.

'Ain't nothin',' Heck said.

'I'm tellin' you,' Tom raised his voice. 'Them's my saddle-bags an' my brother had 'em with 'im this mornin'.'

'You ain't implyin' that Heck here stole the damn bags, are you?' the older man said.

'I'm jus' sayin',' Tom said.

The third man left his horse and joined them. 'What's goin' on?'

Heck pushed Tom aside, put his foot in the stirrup and started to swing himself up into the saddle. Tom grabbed him by the arm, making him lurch backwards and almost fall.

'Why, you young punk.' Heck drew his Colt and waved it in Tom's face. 'Don't you know when to back off?'

'I ain't backin', mister. Them's my saddle-bags an' you know it. My brother had 'em this mornin', an' you ain't gived me no answer about what's happened to him.'

'What you sayin' now?' Heck snarled. 'I done somethin' to your brother?'

Their raised voices had begun to attract attention. The men who had been eating and drinking got up and walked towards them. Dixie stood looking down from the wagon. Frenchie put down the packing-case he had been holding.

A tall, muscular man, with a thick beard under his chin pushed his way through the crowd. He spoke with strength and authority.

'Now, you put that gun away, friend,' he commanded. 'We don' want no shootin' here.'

'Who the hell are you?' the older man snapped. 'You keep outa this.'

'I'm Zac Johnson, leader of the Miners' Committee. I'm the nearest thing there is to law aroun' here. I ain't seen you or your boys before, but I've known young Tom Hope for a while. He ain't one to be pickin' no fight for no good reason.'

'Well damn, if it ain't the leader of the Miners' Committee,' Heck sneered. 'Well, you kin jus' crawl back down your hole in the ground while I deal with this.' He waved his gun dangerously in Zac's direction and started to pull himself up into the saddle again.

Everyone jumped at the crash of a shotgun being fired in the air. Dixie stood on top of the wagon with a scatter-gun in her hands. 'Now,' she bellowed, 'you bin told to put that gun away. So, do it.'

Heck's anger boiled over. His face was twisted with fury.

'Ain't nobody tellin' me nothin',' he snarled, 'let alone no saloon belle.'

He swung his pistol in Dixie's direction. There was another shot. Heck doubled over clutching his arm. His Colt dropped to the ground. Tom stood there with his father's old five-shot pistol in his hand.

The older man took charge. He shoved Heck up on to his horse, tore the saddle-bags loose and flung them on the ground. He snatched up Heck's gun, mounted his own horse and shouted at Buck to do the same.

'We're outa here fer now,' he yelled. 'But you crossed the line, Tom Hope. You winged my boy Heck. If he or his brother don't do nothing about it, then I will. This is Jack

Cheetham an' his boys yer dealin' with here.'

He wheeled his horse round and the three men galloped out of town without looking back.

2

Tom tore open the saddle-bags and thrust his hand inside, checking and rechecking to see if they were truly empty.

Zac said, 'You missing something there, Tom? You've turned white as a ghost.'

'No. It ain't nothin'. Has anyone see Jeb? He was comin' in to take the stage into San Francisco this mornin'.'

'Stage left over an hour ago,' Zac said. 'Can't say I saw Jeb get on it.'

Will Short, the clerk from the Pony Express office ran over to them.

'Rider brought this in a week ago,' he said, catching his breath. 'I bin meanin' to pin it up.'

He held out a yellow poster for them to see. Tom read aloud: 'Wanted. Dead or Alive. John Cheetham, known as "Black Jack" Cheetham, leader of the Cheetham Gang, together with his sons Hector "Heck" Cheetham and Buck Cheetham for robbery and arson at the California State Bank, Wells Fargo Bank and California Port Authority.'

'I knowed I recognized 'em from somewhere,' Will said, hopping from foot to foot. 'Look at that picture. That's

Black Jack Cheetham an' his boys, clear as day.' He pointed to a smudged engraving of three angry-looking men. 'What's it say about a reward?'

Tom continued reading: 'Seven hundred and fifty dollar Reward. Two hundred and fifty dollars per man for arrest and conviction of the robbers. Dead or Alive.'

Zac looked unhappy. 'That's all we need. With the gold runnin' out, we have to work twice as hard as we did. Now we got the Cheethams on our backs as well.'

Another miner joined them. 'I saw 'em in the store coupla hours ago. They was buyin' panning equipment. Said they was headed up to Honey River. I told 'em that's Paiute country up there. Indians don' take kindly to no prospectin' on account Honey River runs through one o' their burial grounds. They git mighty sore about that. That's why prospectors have left that pass alone. They didn't pay me no mind though. Said it took more than a few Injuns to throw a scare into them.'

Will's eyes were popping with excitement. 'I keep my scattergun under the counter ready and loaded, yes sir. If the Cheethams come for me, I'll be ready for 'em. Might even claim the *re*-ward.'

'Well, you better get an extra barrel for that scattergun of yours. There's three of 'em, remember?' Zac said.

'Listen to this,' Tom said. He continued reading. 'All officers are urged to use the utmost caution when making an arrest.'

'Damn,' Will said. 'What do they mean "officers are urged", Zac?'

Zac snorted. 'We ain't got no officers. Never have had.'

'I was gonna put this up in the Pony Express office,' Will said. 'But maybe that ain't such a good idea.'

'I'll take it,' Dixie called from the top of the wagon. 'I'll put it up in the saloon. That way folks will have to come in to take a look at it.'

Tom searched White Fir for Jeb. No one had seen him. The man at the hardware store, which also sold Butterfield Stage tickets, was adamant that Jeb had not bought a ticket that morning.

'What's he wanta go down there fer, anyway? They're putting' store prices up so high now, it ain't hardly worth the cost of a ticket. You kin buy everythin' you want here.'

Tom decided Jeb must have hitched a ride on a wagon to save the cost of the stagecoach fare. He couldn't find anyone who had seen a wagon pull out, but the coming and going of freight wagons was a common enough occurrence for no one to have remarked on it. As there were no letters for him at the Pony Express office, Tom decided to head back up to the claim and continue working.

The mountain path gave a good view over the valley and the road which snaked up to White Fir from Sacremento. Two years ago, one stage a week ran along the road to the mining settlements. Now there were two a day. Tom could make out the dust cloud of an approaching stagecoach way down in the valley. This one would call at White Fir then go on to Placerville.

From his vantage point, Tom spotted a group of riders following less than half a mile behind the stage. He couldn't see how many at first, but a feeling in his gut told him that there were three. The stage driver hadn't seen them yet or he would have slowed to let them pass. The stage was about two miles from White Fir, down the winding mountain road. Tom followed the road with his eye. A pine was down at a hairpin bend a mile outside the town. It was just too much of a coincidence.

There was no way Tom could alert the driver from here. It would take too long to go back to White Fir to get help. He could make it down to the tree blocking the road, if he ran straight down the hillside. If he could shift it, the stage could roll on into White Fir without stopping.

Tom leapt down the mountainside like a wildcat. He stumbled over stones, rocks and boxthorn bushes but somehow managed to remain upright. He staggered on to the road at the hairpin, his lungs bursting. He heaved at the huge pine. It wouldn't budge. The stage arrived within minutes. The Cheethams had closed on it and were keeping pace a few yards behind.

The driver reined in the horses just as the first shot from Jack Cheetham's gun echoed round the valley. The stagecoach guard took a bullet in the back and dropped like a stone before he could lift his shotgun off his lap. He tumbled off his seat and hit the ground hard. His shotgun landed beside him.

Tom had his father's old Manhattan Firearms Company pistol stuffed in his belt, but he knew it was useless at a range greater than the width of a card table. He slipped away into the woods at the side of the road. The Cheethams hadn't seen him. In the confusion, the stage driver, a grizzled old-timer, noticed him and assumed he was the member of the gang who had dragged the pine in the path of the coach.

Hidden behind the undergrowth, Tom watched helplessly as the two passengers, both young women, were made to climb out of the coach, empty their purses and hand over their jewellery. The driver shook with fear. His eyes were riveted to the body of the dead guard. He handed his pocket watch to Black Jack Cheetham without being asked.

'We didn't realize you ladies was aboard,' Black Jack announced with exaggerated politeness. 'I mus' say it's bin a pleasure doin' business with you.'

The women glared at him. They were both barely twenty, one brunette and one blonde. The brunette had dark, intelligent eyes and a pretty face. Her nose had been broken some time ago and had healed flat, like a boxer's. The blonde twisted her hands nervously and stared at the ground, avoiding the gaze of the men. Her hair was the colour of corn and her skin was as pale as china.

'Callin' us ladies an' all don't cut nothin' with us,' the brunette said angrily. 'I'm Lisa May an' this here's Gracie. An' if you had any human feelin's in you, mister, you wouldn't be takin' our hard-earned possessions and leavin' us stranded in the middle of nowhere.'

Jack laughed. 'Well now, you min' tellin me jus' what you two doves is doin' in this part of the Sierras anyhow?'

'First, mister, we ain't no soiled doves. An' you kin git that straight. Second, we're artistes headin' up to the new saloon at White Fir where we'll be workin'. An' it's a damn shame for you to pick on defenceless women like this.'

The Cheethams roared with laughter.

'Ain't met a saloon gal yet you could call defenceless,' Heck said. 'We'll be visitin' you in that saloon, won't we, Pa?'

'Reckon we will,' Black Jack said. 'Come on, boys, let's clear the road for 'em. That means you, Buck. You kin do yer brother's share now he's bin shot.'

Scowling, Buck dismounted and helped his father haul

the pine trunk to one side of the road.

Tom saw his chance. He burst out from the undergrowth and made a dive for the shotgun. One of the women screamed. The stage driver saw Tom coming. Still believing he was part of the gang, the driver launched a kick at Tom which caught him in the temple. Tom's head rang and a shower of phosphorous stars exploded like fireworks in front of his eyes. The Cheethams dropped the pine. Jack and Buck drew their Colts. Tom lay with his face in the dust beside the body of the dead stage guard.

Tom lay still. His shirt was torn at the shoulder. Blood and dirt were raked along the side of his face.

Lisa May, standing next to the driver, saw what had happened.

'You damn fool driver,' she yelled. She swung back her fist in its black-lace glove and socked him with a mighty right-hand punch. The old-timer's knees jellified and he slid slowly down the side of the coach.

'Whoo-ee,' whistled Black Jack. 'Now we're havin' us a party.'

'See what I mean about saloon girls,' Heck said admiringly.

'Damn lucky for him you boys jus' stole my rings,' Lisa May said. 'Or he'd be spittin' teeth.'

'Where did he spring from?' Heck said, pointing to Tom. It took a moment, then he recognized him. 'Wait a minute, it's that young fella took a shot at me. Grab ahold of 'im, Buck.'

Buck hauled Tom to his feet and pinned his arms behind him. Heck yanked the pistol out of Tom's belt and tossed it aside. With his good arm, he heaved two straight punches at Tom's belly and then slammed another into his cheek. Tom slumped forward and Buck let him fall. Tom lay moaning on the dirt road. Buck spat a mouthful of phlegm at him for good measure.

'We jus' bin up to that two-bit mineshaft o' yours, lookin' for you,' Heck crowed. 'Left you a little present. Lucky for you, that little popgun o' yours ain't give me no more'n a scratch or you'd be buzzard meat by now.' He turned to Black Jack. 'Come on, Pa. Let's git this tree shifted an' get outa here.'

With the pine trunk by the side of the road, the Cheethams mounted up.

'Might have to drive the stage yourself, ladies. Seeing as how you knocked out the driver,' Black Jack laughed.

'Don't you worry about that,' Lisa May said. 'We'll have the fool back on his feet in no time.'

As soon as the Cheethams were gone, Lisa May rushed over to comfort Tom. The other girl, Gracie, slapped the driver until he woke up. They helped Tom into the stage with them and the driver pulled himself painfully up on to his seat. Lisa May collected Tom's pistol and the guard's shotgun.

'You kin come back for him later,' she sneered at the driver, indicating the guard. 'Whole lotta use he was.'

As the stage jogged up to White Fir, the girls compared notes.

Gracie said: 'You lose anythin' of value?'

'Hell no.' Lisa May grinned. 'I keep my valuable trinkets in my drawers. An' if any sonofabitch finds them down there, well, I reckon I've lost everything anyway.'

Up at White Fir, Dixie's huge saloon tent was partly put up. Frenchie was overseeing a group of men who were hammering in the pegs and tightening the guys. As payment, Dixie had promised them a dance with one of the girls. As the stage drew up a crowd gathered to listen to the young women tell their story.

'Well, it's damn good to see y'all,' Dixie said.

Zac wrote out a notice calling a meeting of the Miners' Committee the following day to discuss what to do about outlaws. Willy nailed it to the door of the Pony Express office. Then the two of them borrowed Dixie's wagon and drove down the hill to pick up the body of the stage guard.

Lisa May bathed Tom's face. Dixie promised to stand him a whiskey when the saloon opened.

Tom asked the crowd if anyone had seen Jeb. No one had.

3

Tom slept at the saloon tent and stayed at White Fir the following day. Since he'd pulled his gun on Heck Cheetham, Dixie had taken a liking to him. She offered him two dollars and a meal for a day's work helping to set up the saloon. Tom accepted. It meant he could keep an eye out for Jeb.

In the evening Tom met Doc Morgan strolling down from his cabin. His collecting bag was over his shoulder as usual. It contained a few botanical specimens and two bottles of his home-made tanglefoot. 'A sample for the saloon lady. See if she wants to put in an order, wholesale. Other one's jus' to remin' me what it tastes like,' he added with a wink.

Tom was overjoyed when Doc told him Jeb was safe. Doc said he had removed most of the shot from Jeb's thigh. 'Two more uses for my fine whiskey,' he said. 'Takes the patient's mind off things an' cleans up a wound real nice. Ain't no bugs can survive a splash of hooch.'

The Miners' Committee meeting was long and noisy. Dixie had let Zac use the saloon tent. Gracie and Lisa May had started selling drinks before the meeting, which led to heckling and interruptions. The committee members sat round a trestle-table at the front. Zac kept order by shouting down the hecklers. Eventually, by a show of hands, the miners decided to send someone down to Sacramento to put the word out that a bounty hunter was needed to deal with the Cheethams. But their real worry was the Paiute Indians.

Over the years, relations between the Paiute and the miners had often been strained. Streams diverted for panning had ruined salmon runs which the Paiute relied on; open-cast mining had decimated woodland; shafts had damaged root systems. The miners who had been in the mountains longest remembered Indian attacks provoked by their abuse of the landscape.

Word was that the Paiute were becoming angry again. Gold fever made men careless of the damage they were doing. The explosion in the number of miners had pushed the Indians into higher and more remote areas of the Sierra Nevada. Hydraulic-mining companies were beginning to operate in the north. The new immigrants had no respect for Paiute traditions.

The White Fir miners had always left the Honey River area untouched and this had enabled them to live peacefully, if uneasily, alongside the Paiute. Now, the Cheethams had gone panning for gold in a burial ground. The miners were right to be worried.

The only person who was able to communicate with the tribe was Doc Morgan. He was always consulted when something concerning the Indians came up. The Paiute trusted him because he had learned enough of their language to be able to communicate. The present chief's father had got to know him before the miners came.

Doc and Tom stood at the back of the meeting. 'I could go up to Honey River,' Doc said at last. 'Try to make contact with the tribe. Though I kin tell you, if they don' wanna talk to me, I won't be able to find 'em. I could try an' tell 'em that the damn Cheethams ain't nothing to do with us. But if they're messin' with sacred ground, there'll be some young Paiute braves who'll want their scalps. Once they get a taste for that, then it's just a matter of time 'fore they turn on the rest of us.'

Zac looked worried. 'If that happens, then the army'll come in an' that'll kick off an all-out Indian war. You kin kiss goodbye to goldminin' then.'

The meeting fell silent. Then Dixie's musical voice rang out. She stood at the side of the meeting cradling her ginger cat in her arms. 'Whatcha shilly-shallyin' round for, boys? The Paiute don't want the Cheethams, we don' want the Cheethams. We'll wait till they come down for supplies, then we'll keep 'em here and give 'em over to the bounty hunter.'

'Why d'we need a bounty hunter?' someone called. 'We could claim that two hundred and fifty dollars a head ourselves.'

'That's plumb crazy,' someone else shouted. 'Who's gonna be the one calls out Black Jack Cheetham an' his boys? We're miners, we ain't gunslingers. Them Cheethams will plug you stone dead soon as look at you.'

'That's just it,' a third man called. 'Those Cheethams ain't like us. They ain't miners. They ain't got the patience to pan fer gold. They're gonna get fed up and start to reckon it's easier to steal our gold rather than find their own. I bet they done that already. Anyone here been robbed since the Cheethams bin here?'

There was a pause and no one spoke up.

'Damnit,' the man continued angrily. 'Nobody won't say nothing even if he has bin robbed, because that would mean telling everyone that he's made a strike. We're all so damn secretive, ain't we?'

Tom wondered if the Cheethams had found the gold Jeb had been carrying. Doc hadn't mentioned it.

Back at the doc's cabin, Tom flung his arms round Jeb. He was so relieved to see his brother, he was hardly able to sit still long enough for Doc to bathe his eye. Doc gave him a concoction to drink and a packet of herbs soaked in whiskey to hold over his bruised face. They told Jeb about the Miners' Committee, about the bounty hunter and about no one admitting to being robbed. Jeb kept quiet about what had happened to him until they were on the track back to their camp and out of Doc's hearing.

'You didn't tell Doc nothin' about the gold?' Tom said.

' 'Course I didn't. That gold's for Pa an' the farm. That's why we gotta get it back.' Jeb hesitated. 'You ain't wrathy with me, are you Tom? I couldn't do nothin'. Nex' time I see them sonsabitches I'm gonna get that gold back, I swear.'

'I ain't mad. You're my brother, Jeb. When I thought something had happened to you, I was so balled up I didn't know what to do.'

Jeb had made a crutch for himself. Progress up the steep track was slow. When they reached the spot where Jeb had been robbed, Tom scrambled down the scree to retrieve the shotgun.

As soon as Tom and Jeb got to the claim, they knew instantly that something was wrong. Boss wasn't there to greet them. They hadn't chained him up, but he never went far. Then they thought that their tent had blown down. It took a moment for them to realize that the guys had been cut. Their possessions were scattered around like autumn leaves.

With a sick feeling swimming in their guts, they walked over to the entrance of the mine. The props had been pulled away and the roof and walls had collapsed. The slope above it was sunken in, so the collapse must go far back down the shaft. They wouldn't be able to tell how far until they started digging. They knew they were faced with weeks of work to clear away the rubble, cut new props and make the shaft safe. Jack remembered Heck Cheetham's words about leaving a present for them.

As they stared in shocked disbelief at the heap of broken rock where the mouth of the shaft had been, they noticed a movement in the trees on the slope above. Boss was swinging by his neck from a length of wire. Tom and Jeb fell over each other, crying his name, scrambling up the slope to cut him down. The companionable terrier had been shot in the head.

Neither of them could speak. They each held Boss in their arms for a while, but his body was stiff and cold and felt strange to them. They dug his grave and buried him in silence, in the shade of a scrub oak. Jeb hid his face so that his elder brother would not see his tears.

An old-timer had given Boss to them the day they arrived in Sacramento. He had been heading down to San Francisco and then back to New York by steamship and wasn't sure that he would be allowed to take him on board. Rather than risk having to let him loose in the port, he gave him to Tom and Jeb. Boss had been their faithful companion ever since.

'I dunno about this bounty hunter,' Tom said later, trying to distract Jeb from thinking about Boss.

They had put up the tent, got their possessions back into some sort of order and brewed up a pot of coffee. They sat on the hard ground leaning back against a tree trunk.

'Even if he finds the Cheethams and gets the gold, how do we know he ain't gonna steal it an' say he never found it?'

'It could take weeks,' Jeb added. 'Cheethams coulda spent it all by then.'

'Think we could go after 'em,' Tom said. 'Try 'n' get the gold back?'

Jeb looked nervous. 'We got one old shotgun an' one pistol that don't shoot straight. The Cheethams are panning in the Honey River which is about ten miles across country and we ain't got no horses.'

'In that case, we're gonna sit here and spend the next month clearing out the mineshaft and shoring it all up again. Then there's a just a chance that we might find some more gold.'

'I dunno. . . .' Jeb said.

'There was enough gold there to buy at least half the farm outright. It woulda got the bank off our backs, I know it would.' Tom said. Then he added, 'Look, Jeb, to my way o' thinkin', we ain't got no choice. There ain't no chance of us findin' a seam like that again.'

A breath of chill mountain wind lifted the leaves on the oak trees around them. Tom and Jeb shivered.

'We gotta go after the Cheethams. We'll borrow the money, go down to Sacramento. We'll buy guns and hire horses.'

'Borrow the money? Who's gonna lend us the money? We ain't told a soul about the gold we found. Now, no one's gonna believe we've got any,' Jeb said.

'No. Not a loan,' Tom said. 'We'll get someone to put up a grubstake in the claim. We own the claim, don't we? We'll take a loan against a percentage of what we find in the future.'

'Who's gonna put up a percentage when they don't believe we got any gold and the shaft is in ruins anyway?'

'Doc Morgan might.'

'Doc?'

'He'd help us if he could.'

'He'd help us if he could stay sober long enough.'

Next morning they told Doc Morgan everything. He sat at the table in his cabin and scratched his beard. When Tom had finished the story, Doc took a cob pipe from his pocket and stuffed it full of home-grown tobacco leaves. He drew deeply and exhaled a stream of blue smoke.

'Why d'ya come to me?' he asked.

'We figured you might believe us,' Jeb said.

The doc grunted.

'What makes ya think I got enough money to put up a stake?'

'We was just hopin' you have.'

Doc grunted again. A cloud of smoke billowed around him.

'Well,' he said at last. 'If you're thinkin' of goin' over Honey River way, you're gonna need me along. You can't just ride on in there, not without makin' the Paiute mad as hell. If they git angry with ya, ya gonna end up crowbait. That's fer sure. An' you gonna have to talk to 'em, explain what you're doin'. Then there's just a chance that they might let you in an' might not kill ya. If Jack Cheetham an' his boys are messin' with the Honey River, them Paiute braves are gonna be mad already.' He looked at Tom. 'An' I'll put up a grubstake. Cost of guns and hire of horses against ten per cent of the claim.' He held out his hand.

Tom and Jeb whooped with delight. Each of them shook Doc's hand in turn to seal the deal.

'Don't you go cowboy-whoopin' yet,' Doc warned. 'I ain't sure we kin pull this off. But it's worth a try. Now, we kin drink to success with a mug o' my firewater an' wish ourselves luck. We're sure gonna need it. That's about all we kin do fer now. Then you boys kin stay here an' decide who's goin down to Sacramento to git the guns an' horses.'

Doc disappeared out of the cabin to wherever it was he hid his money.

4

It was a bright, spring morning as Tom, Jeb and Doc set off across country in the direction of Honey River. The mountain air was crisp on their faces and the pale sunlight had yet to warm the day. Tom and Jeb pulled their woollen jackets tight around them. Doc had his rabbit-skin cape over his shoulders, the reward of a trade with the Paiute. His specimen bag was underneath it. Jeb had packed supplies. Tom had brought good coffee up from Sacramento along with horses hired for a month, shotguns and Navy Colts for himself and Jeb.

The horses picked their way over the stony ground. Birdsfoot ferns, bright-yellow columbines and pale monkey flowers grew between the rocks. Silver streams dashed down the slopes. On the higher ground above them, ponderosa pines and white firs guarded the valleys.

Doc began to tell stories about the old days. He described how he had been the first man to build a cabin on the mountain, about how the Paiute had been amazed to find him there and how they had welcomed him to one of their villages. They had been amused by the interest he took in the way they lived and in their medicine. The old chief and the elders of the tribe had befriended him and he had been able to learn some of their language.

But things changed when the miners poured in in 'forty nine. The mountainsides became despoiled and ancient streams were diverted. There were skirmishes between Paiute braves and drunken miners who had blundered into Paiute camps either by accident or on purpose. Paiute women had been threatened. Tribal chiefs heard rumours of the white men's army fighting wars against other tribes east of the Rockies. Doc was suddenly no longer welcome at the Indian camps. But some of the braves still came to him to trade whiskey.

'Brought some trade goods with me, some o' my fire-water as well,' Doc said. 'Might have to bribe our way in to Honey River.'

At midday they stopped in a clearing to rest the horses and brew some coffee. They leaned back against the trunks of mountain maples. The sunlight played through the bright-green leaves and a stream ran over its stony bed. A black-tailed deer peered at them through the under-growth and skittered away.

'I knowed the fellas you bought your claim off,' Doc said. 'They was English fellas. Reckoned they'd mined for tin back home. Weren't no good at it though. Superstitious as hell too. They couldn't seem to make the roof of the entrance to the shaft secure. It was always falling in on 'em. Blamed the tommyknockers. Said they was little fellas who lived in the mine who would play tricks on 'em. They'd hide their tools, stuff like that. You could hear 'em knockin' on the walls of a shaft just before there was going to be a collapse. Then these little guys would shoot outa the mine like lightning 'cross a summer sky.

Never got trapped themselves.'

'What happened to 'em?'

'The tommyknockers?'

Tom laughed. 'No. The English guys.'

'Got fed up with the roof fallin' in on 'em. Said they was goin' to open a store in San Francisco an' sell picks an' shovels to people as they got off the boat. Easy money, they reckoned.'

'Sure easier than diggin' for a livin',' Jeb said.

'You know they salted the claim a little before they sold it to you,' Doc said.

'We worked that one out,' Tom said. 'They weren't too bright, them guys. They left a few flecks of dust round the entrance, so's you couldn't miss it, but it weren't nowhere else in the shaft. Didn't make no difference though,' he added. 'It was the only claim we could afford.'

Tom poured cups of coffee and handed them round with some hardtack biscuits. Doc paused.

'You ever heard the tommyknockers?' he asked seriously.

'Sure have,' Jeb said. 'Tom says I ain't though.'

Tom raised his eyes, unwilling to be drawn.

'I was down the shaft, one day. Months ago now. My flame went out. I musta knocked it over or somethin'. Anyhow, while I was feelin' round for it in the dark, I heard this knockin'. Slow it was at first. Then it got faster, like someone was in a real hurry. I lit the flame and dang me, I looked up and the prop right in front of me was split. I jammed another one in there fast, you bet. Another minute and the roof woulda bin down on top o' me.' Jeb grinned. 'It was the tommyknockers warned me, see?'

'I heard stories like that before,' Doc reflected.

'Stories,' Tom snorted. 'That's the right word for 'em.'

'Jus' because you never heard 'em, you think they don't exist,' Jeb said. 'That ain't right.'

'All right, all right,' Tom said. 'We had this argument a thousand times. I ain't sayin' nothin'.' He got to his feet and walked over to the horses.

Suddenly, there was a sharp sound, like an axe biting into a log. Something struck the tree trunk some way above their heads. They looked up. An arrow with black tail feathers was sticking out of the trunk.

'Hell,' Jeb breathed. 'They seen us and we ain't even there yet.'

Tom started to slide a shotgun out from where it had been tied to the saddle. Doc saw him.

'No,' he hissed. 'Put that back. They're just telling us they're here.'

Doc put out his hand to silence Tom. He called out something in Paiute language. There was a pause. Tom and Jeb took their lead from Doc and stayed perfectly still.

Doc called out again. To Tom and Jeb, it sounded like the language of birds. They waited again.

A young man stepped out from behind a stand of live oaks a few yards away. He wore a buckskin cape over his shoulders, rows of bright beads round his neck, a buckskin loincloth and moccasins. He carried a bow in his hands with an arrow slotted into it, ready to fire. Doc said something again. The man answered briefly and lowered his bow.

The Paiute stared at them. Tom and Jeb sensed that he noticed everything about them, their horses, their guns. They made no movement. The Indian spoke again.

'He wants to know what we're doing here. He says we

frightened away the deer.'

'Whatcha tell 'im?' Jeb said anxiously.

'I said we wanted to ask if we could go across Paiute country to the Honey River. Hush now. He's gotta think what to do,' Doc whispered.

The Paiute brave spoke again.

'He wants to know how come I know his language.'

In one deft, split-second movement, the brave lifted his bow to his shoulder and fired.

Tom threw himself to the ground. Jeb yelled and clutched Doc. A few yards behind them a young black-tailed deer fell to the ground, shot through the heart. The brave waved them aside and strode towards the body of the animal. He pulled out his arrow, returned it to his quiver and heaved the carcass up on to his shoulder. Before making his way back into the woods, he said something else to Doc.

'He wants us to wait here,' Doc said.

They sat where they were and spoke only in whispers for half an hour.

'You sure kin speak that Paiute language good,' Tom said admiringly.

'I'm outa practice,' Doc said. 'When the old chief was alive, he had the medicine man teach me. Then the old chief used to like to hear me try to say somethin'. I could get the right words but I used to say 'em wrong. He used to roll about like a big old bear, laughing his head off.'

Without warning, the Paiute brave appeared again. None of them had heard him approach. He said a single sharp word to Doc.

Doc turned to the others. 'C'mon.'

They followed the brave across the wooded hillside,

along a narrow deer track through the undergrowth. He walked quickly, never looking round to see if they were keeping up. After a mile, the ground levelled and the woodland opened on to a wide, grassy clearing.

Four tepees made of strips of tree-bark and wood, tied up against conical frames, stood around the smouldering remains of a fire. There were a few people about. A group of young women were skinning rabbits and throwing carcasses in to one basket and pelts into another. Another woman, with dark smears of charcoal on her cheeks and forehead, sat apart from the others, intent on sorting through a pile of wild garlic. Three children sat near her playing a dice game with plum stones. A young man was stretching a deer hide on to a frame. Everyone froze when the men entered the camp. They stared at them without either hostility or warmth.

'Jus' keep quiet and move slow,' Doc whispered. 'It's all right, they've invited us here.'

Two older men emerged from one of the tepees. They wore buckskin cloaks like the brave, and buckskin leggings. The brave motioned Doc, Tom and Jeb to sit on the ground in front of the older men. As soon as they sat down the Indians sat too.

One of the older Paiute started speaking. Doc translated. 'He says his name is Liwanu, which means 'growl of a bear'. He is the chief of this band of Paiute. He remembers his father talking about me, that is why he wanted to meet us. He wants to know what presents we have brought him.'

Jeb looked anxiously at Tom. Doc smiled, felt inside the specimen bag he wore round his shoulder and produced four small paper packets. He tore one open and showed

Chief Liwanu that they contained sewing needles. Liwanu nodded solemn approval. Then Doc produced more packets. These contained differently coloured beads. Again the chief nodded. Last of all, Doc brought out a bottle of his homemade firewater. The chief nodded again.

'I'm gonna ask him if he'll let us ride through to Honey River,' Doc whispered.

Liwanu looked at him hard. The second man spoke and Doc translated quickly.

'Honey River runs through sacred burial grounds. The people from White Fir know this. Up until now they have stayed away from Honey River and in return the Paiute people have not objected when the whites attacked the forests and the mountain sides in the search for the metal that is precious to them. No white man is to go to Honey River. You must return to White Fir by the way you came.'

The chief stood up, picked up the packets of beads and needles and took them over to the group of women. He took the bottle of Doc's whiskey, pulled out the cork with his teeth and upended it so the brown liquid poured out over the ground where he stood. When the bottle was empty he nodded sharply to the brave who had brought them to the camp. He took Doc by the arm and led him back the way he had come. Tom and Jeb followed close behind. As they left, they heard the camp return to normal. The women began chatting. The children started to laugh over their game.

The brave led them back to their horses and then melted back into the woods.

'Damn,' Jeb said. 'What do we do now?'

'Only one thing to do,' Doc said. 'We hightail it back to

White Fir and don' come back here no more.'

'Can't we find another way through?' Tom said.

'We're on Paiute territory. They've told us to leave, so we do. Right now.' Doc was emphatic.

'What about the Cheethams?'

'Well, if we don' get 'em, sure as hell the Paiute will. Now, come on.'

The three men mounted their horses and urged them back through the forest.

It was evening when they emerged from the woodland a few hundred yards above White Fir. The sun was going down over the pines away on the peaks to the west. The collection of ramshackle buildings, dirty white tents and wagons was a welcome sight. The biggest tent of all was the new saloon. Even though most of the flooring and furniture had not yet been brought up from Sacramento, they could see it was open for business. As they rode down the hillside, they could hear Dixie's rich contralto voice booming out a rendition of 'Sweet Betsy from Pike' with someone banging out an accompaniment on an out-of-tune piano. When the song ended, the sound of applause, whistles and stamping feet filled the evening air.

5

A wooden sign, hanging from the top of the tent pole, announced BON TON SALOON in large red capitals. The sound of conversation and laughter came from inside. Tom pulled back the canvas flap.

The place was lit in golden halos of light from candles in bottles at the centre of each table. A row of oil lamps with fancy glass shades stood at each end of the three long trestles which had been set up end to end as a makeshift bar. Crates of whiskey were stacked behind it. Gracie stood ready to serve drinks. Lisa May was sitting at one of the tables talking to the men.

At the far end of the tent, wooden tabletops had been laid on the ground as a makeshift dance floor. A piano stood to one side. Frenchie was banker at an intense game of faro at one of the corner tables. Dixie stood in the middle of the tent surveying the proceedings. She was dressed in a green silken gown, her red hair piled up French style and decorated with ribbons. She cradled her sleeping ginger tomcat at her ample bosom. She noticed Tom, Doc and Jeb as soon as they entered.

'Guns at the door, boys,' Dixie called in a sing-song

voice and nodded towards a table with an array of shotguns propped against it and a pile of pistols on top. A piece of board leant against it which read: Leave Your Guns Here signed D. Spinette. Tom and Jeb unbuckled their gunbelts and Doc propped his shotgun against the others.

'I'm gonna stand you a drink,' Dixie said to Tom. 'Some sucker had the brass nerve to wave a gun at me and this young fella took a shot at him,' she announced to the assembled company.

A few of the miners looked up admiringly. 'I'd have shot 'im for you, Dixie,' someone called out. Others laughed good-naturedly.

'You always carry that cat aroun'?' Jeb asked curiously.

'This here's Ted,' Dixie explained. 'My granpappy gived 'im to me. Named 'im Ted after the ol' boy cus he likes to sleep in the afternoons, jus' like granpappy did.'

Jeb went to stroke the sleeping tom. 'Don't you do that,' Dixie warned sharply, pulling away. 'Ted don' like no one to stroke 'im 'cept me.'

'Sorry, Dixie,' Jeb said.

'S'all right. You weren't to know,' she said. 'Now, let's get young Tom Hope here a drink. You boys drinkin' too?' She nodded to the girl behind the bar who poured Tom a whiskey.

'You gonna sing another song, Dixie?' Doc asked.

'If someone buys me a drink. Cost you twenty cents. Pay Gracie at the bar an' I'll have the drink later.'

'Know "Clementine"?' Doc asked. 'That's my favourite.'

'Sure do,' Dixie said. 'I'll sing her in a minute. Gotta give my piano player a rest jus' now.' She smiled graciously at Doc and swept off to encourage more of her patrons to buy drinks for the girls.

In the meantime, Doc headed over for the faro table. 'Even money on all bets,' Frenchie said as he approached. 'Bank pays four to one on the last turn. Will you be joining us, sir?'

'Like to.' Doc grinned. 'Ain't played a game o' faro since I dunno when. Ain't got no money though. You take a bottle of whiskey for a two-dollar bet?'

Frenchie laughed. 'This here's a saloon, mister. We got whiskey. Got any gold? We'll take that.'

'Ain't a miner,' Doc said, disappointed.

'That's all right, friend. You kin jus' draw up a chair an' watch awhile. Then you kin come back when you got some money with you.'

Doc took the second bottle of tanglefoot out of his bag, eased out the cork and took a deep slug. Frenchie started to deal a card at a time from the box. The players watched intently.

Lisa May sat down at the piano and began the opening bars of 'Clementine'. There was a murmur of approval from the drinkers. Dixie took up a position beside her and started to sing, still holding the ginger cat to her breast. She took the song slowly and with great passion. Her silky contralto filled the air and every eye was upon her. The drinkers put down their glasses, Frenchie paused in the middle of dealing the cards, Gracie stopped serving drinks at the bar. Every heart was touched by the tragedy of the story the song told, made beautiful by Dixie's voice.

When she came to the end, Dixie repeated the first verse. All the men in the saloon sang softly along with her, making a pillow of sound on which Dixie's velvet voice rested. Some had their eyes closed, maybe thinking of home. Others quickly brushed away a tear. Everyone watched the songstress as she transported them for a moment out of White Fir, away from their mineshafts and their hard daily lives to a place of beauty and peace.

When the thunderous applause died down, the players looked to the faro game and the drinkers began to pick up their glasses. Gradually, the men began to realize that Dixie had her gaze fixed on the saloon entrance. Every one turned to look. The Cheethams stood there with their arms folded, taking in the scene with hard, cynical eyes.

Black Jack was the first to speak. 'Mighty nice singin', ma'am But me an' my boys ain't come into town to listen to no songbird We come to do some drinkin', on accounta we struck it rich, yes sir.'

Everyone turned towards them.

'We been pannin' up on Honey River,' Black Jack announced. 'You White Fir boys missed out on somethin', I kin tell you. Some fool told us not to go up there on accounta it bein' Injun ground. Well, we ain't seen hide nor hair of an Injun since we been there.' Black Jack laughed. 'Anyways, if we had seen one o' them savages, we woulda shot 'im an his bow an' arrow all to hell.' He turned to Gracie at the bar. 'Now, c'mon pretty thing, you reach around an' fin' us a bottle o' whiskey an' three glasses.'

'Wait.' Dixie's voice rang from far end of the saloon. 'No guns in here, mister. You seen the sign.'

'I ain't seen no sign, nowhere,' Black Jack replied innocently. 'You see a sign, boys?'

The Cheetham boys sniggered obligingly. Heck lazily reached down, picked up the board which said: Leave Your Guns Here and threw it casually out of the tent into the night.

'Now gimmie that whiskey, girl,' Jack growled. 'An' make it quick.'

Gracie hesitated and looked at Dixie. Black Jack pulled his Colt, cocked it and pointed it at Gracie. She screamed and shoved a bottle and glasses across the bar to him.

'Buck, you stay back there by those guns. Heck, you come here and have a drink with your pappy.'

Black Jack poured three full tumblers of whiskey and put the bottle back on the bar.

'Just one more thing, folks' Black Jack announced. 'We got ourselves a new sign. It says 'No one has his gun back till I say so'. Ol' Buck is gonna stan' there to make sure no one can't have their gun back 'fore we leave. An',' he added, 'if anyone does happen to go for a gun, we might jus' have to shoot 'em. Now, y'all git back to yer drinkin'.'

Black Jack downed his whiskey in one gulp and poured himself another. Heck knocked his own drink back and then took a glass over to Buck at the gun table. Black Jack strode across to the faro game.

'Even money on all bets. Bank pays four to one on the last turn,' Frenchie said matter-of-factly.

The other gamblers moved their chairs aside to make room for Black Jack.

Heck leant on the bar and stared at Gracie's breasts. Buck stayed by the gun table. When the song finished, Tom and Jeb walked over to stand by Doc and watch the faro game.

Black Jack looked round at the other players. 'Y'all got money?' he asked.

The miners nodded.

'Bank got money?' Black Jack looked hard at Frenchie.

'Bank's always got money,' Frenchie said. 'What're you

askin fer, mister?'

Black Jack leered. He reached in his pocket and tossed a small leather purse, tied at the neck by a thong, on to the table. Jeb grabbed Tom's arm. It was their bag of gold. Black Jack leaned forward, slowly undid the purse and shook out a few nuggets on to the table. The players gasped.

Black Jack grinned at Frenchie. 'There's my money. Your bank up to this?'

Sensing something was up, Dixie walked over to the table. Frenchie nodded towards the nuggets spilling out of the purse. 'Play 'im, Frenchie,' she said quietly and walked away. Frenchie threw away the soda card and started to deal. Jack dropped the nuggets back into the purse, tied the neck and pushed it back into his pocket.

The atmosphere in the saloon was returning to something like normal. A buzz of conversation was picking up. Dixie told Lisa May to play something on the piano. She began a version of 'My Log Cabin Home' which brought a spattering of applause from the drinkers who recognized the tune. Heck had got through a good deal of the bottle of whiskey by this time and was openly leering at Gracie, who stared resolutely in the opposite direction. Buck had pulled a chair over to the gun table and sat sipping his drink.

After another whiskey, Heck said, 'Whyn't you an' me have a little dance?'

Gracie stared at him contemptuously. 'Can't you see I'm workin?' she said.

'You ain't workin',' Heck countered. 'You're jus' standin' there. Ain't nobody buyin' no drinks right now. C'mon, jus' one dance.'

Buck overheard all this. 'Don' she wanna dance with you, Heck?' he jeered. 'That's right, ma'am,' he called over to Gracie. 'He's too damn ugly to dance with, ain't he?'

'Shaddup Buck,' Heck called.

'An' he's mean,' Heck went on. 'He bought you a drink yet?' Gracie ignored them both. 'I thought so. That boy'd steal a fly off a blind spider. He ain't bought no one a drink since the day he was born.' Buck leaned back on this chair and roared with laughter at his own joke.

'I'm warnin' you, Buck,' Heck hissed.

Gracie stared across the saloon, refusing to look at either of them.

Heck was nonplussed. He swayed slightly, with all the whiskey in his head. 'C'mon missy,' he implored. 'Don' pay no mind to him. He's jus' my brother. He's always joshin' like that. Jus' one dance. I ain't danced with no one since my mama died.' Heck swallowed another whiskey and refilled his glass. 'We used to dance round the cabin when I was a kid. My grandpappy played the fiddle real good.'

'Now shaddup, Heck,' Buck exploded. 'Don't you go talkin' about stuff like 'at. Don't you go talkin' about mama to no saloon whore.'

'That's it,' Gracie snapped. 'I ain't standin' here to be called names by no two-bit prospector, jus' walked in.'

'See what you done now?' Heck said. He leaned across the bar and made a grab for Gracie's arm. She pulled away quickly.

'C'mon, jus' one dance.'

Buck laughed again. The group of miners who were sitting at the nearest table had been watching all this.

Heck suddenly rounded on them.

'What y'all lookin' at?'

'Why, we ain't lookin', mister,' one of them began. He was a thin-faced man with a unkempt beard under his chin. His shirt was torn and dirty.

'What you say? You laughin' at me? You damn well laughin' at me, ain'tcha?'

'No, I ain't,' the man protested.

Heck lurched over to him. The man shoved his chair backwards and stood up quickly to try to get out of Heck's way. Heck swung a wild aimless punch. He knocked himself off balance and collapsed backwards against the bar. The trestle upended. Glasses, bottles and the row of oil lamps smashed. It took a second for pools of burning oil to flow over the ground.

Men at the nearby tables shoved their chairs back. Gracie screamed, pinned against the pile of whiskey crates. Heck lay in a heap of drunken confusion, not realizing what had happened. Buck jumped up and dragged his brother to his feet as flames began to lick their way up the canvas walls of the tent.

Men further down the tent started shouting and running towards the entrance. The gun table was knocked over and the miners shoved and scrabbled on the ground searching for their guns. Buck drew his Colt and fired in the air.

'Y'all leave those guns alone, y'hear?' Buck yelled. The miners nearest the pile of weapons grabbed whatever they could and hurled themselves out into the night. Flames were racing up the walls and across the roof of the tent. Everyone surged towards the entrance.

Frenchie's first thought was to gather up the money

and the cards. 'This way,' he hissed. There was another entrance to the tent behind his chair, tied with strips of canvas. The card players waited for an agonizing second while he undid the laces. He pushed the canvas door aside and led Tom, Jeb and Black Jack Cheetham out into the night. 'Dixie,' he yelled over his shoulder. 'This way.' Dixie and Lisa May gathered up their skirts and followed. Frenchie held open the canvas door for them.

Outside the tent, everyone watched in horror as orange flames reared over the tent roof against the night sky. Men ran round the fire trying to find their friends. Above the shouting, Dixie's voice could be heard calling the names of the girls.

Round the front of the tent, a shotgun went off. There was screaming. Someone had ducked back through the flames and smoke and was throwing out the weapons. The gun went off as it hit the ground and sprayed the crowd with buckshot. Those who had been standing in front rolled on the ground in agony. There was more shoving as a crowd fought over the weapons. Tom pushed through to try to retrieve their Colts. Jeb followed Black Jack Cheetham.

Black Jack pushed through the mêlée in search of his boys. A warning shout went up from the crowd. The guy ropes were alight and the posts were about to fall. The crowd fled. Men tripped over the ropes of other tents in the dark and brought them down. Other men fell on top of them. People were screaming in terror.

One end of the saloon collapsed. The burning pole and canvas crashed down on to the adjoining tents. The fire took hold in seconds. A frenzy of yellow flame danced from tent to tent. A covered wagon caught alight. The terrified horses, bucking and rearing, broke free from the rail where they were tethered and galloped off into the night, towing the flaming wagon behind them. Fifty yards down the street, one of the wheels smashed against a pile of logs. The wagon crashed over on to its side against the wooden wall of the Pony Express office. Men ran up to cut the horses free.

Jeb didn't take his eyes off Jack Cheetham. Black Jack found Heck and Buck near their horses, across the street from the burning saloon. Buck shoved Heck up on to his saddle and mounted up himself. As Black Jack himself had one foot in a stirrup and was about to mount, Jeb called him.

'Hey, mister.'

Black Jack looked round, surprised.

'You got our gold an' you gotta hand it over.'

Black Jack swung himself up into his saddle. 'Who the hell are you?'

'That gold in your pocket. You never panned that. You stole it.'

'Come on, Pa,' Buck said. 'Don' pay him no mind. We gotta get outta here.'

'That's our gold. You hand it over,' Jeb persisted.

Over by what had been the entrance to the saloon, Tom had managed to find their guns. He shouted Jeb's name and looked wildly round for him, but couldn't see him. He shoved his way through the crowd. Another cry went up. The second pole was about to fall. Men panicked. Everyone was running when the pole crashed down on the opposite side, dragging swaths of burning canvas down on the flat roof of the hardware store.

Tom suddenly caught sight of Jeb and started towards

him. Horrified, he realized what Jeb was trying to do. He snatched a gun from its holster as he ran and called out to tell Jeb to back away. Before he could get close enough for Jeb to hear him, he saw Jack Cheetham draw his pistol and shoot Jeb in the chest. Jeb was flung backwards by the force of the shot. Tom yelled. The Cheethams wheeled their horses round and galloped off into the darkness. Tom fired wildly after them. Shot after shot, until the chamber was empty.

Tom flung himself down on his knees beside Jeb.

'I was tryin' to get the gold back, Tom,' Jeb whispered. 'For the farm.'

'You jus' lie still,' Tom said.

'I ain't hurt bad, am I, Tom?' Dark blood was welling in his mouth. Orange light from the burning tents flickered across his face.

'No, you'll be fine. Don't talk now.'

A small group of people gathered round them. Lisa May and Dixie were among them.

'I seed what happened,' a man said. 'Black Jack Cheetham shot him. He weren't even holdin' a gun.'

Jeb sighed suddenly and the life went out of him.

Tom leaned over him and his tears fell on his brother's face. Dixie handed the cat to Lisa May, put her arms round Tom's shoulders and hugged him to her.

'Where's Doc?' Tom said.

6

Zac and the Miners' Committee took charge. A line of men was formed from the spring on the edge of town to the burning saloon tent. Buckets of water were passed along. Another group doused the smouldering walls of the Pony Express office and dragged the burning wagon a safe distance away. Men dismantled their tents and moved their belongings out of reach of the flames. Gradually, they brought the fire under control. The street was clogged with mud and the night air smelled of soot.

Doc had been asleep on the ground, a few yards outside the saloon tent, until someone tripped over him. His empty whiskey bottle was still clenched in his fist. He staggered around in the crowd looking for Tom and Jeb. Eventually, someone from the Miners' Committee stood him in the bucket line. When the remains of the saloon tent were safely soaked and the line broke up, he came across Dixie sitting in the darkness with her arms around Tom. After a while she left him and went off to find her girls. Doc sat with Tom until first light.

Tom lay slumped against Doc. All his strength was gone. He just wanted to pick Jeb up, to tell him everything was fine. Tom's whole body trembled with the shock that came from deep inside him. Doc held on to him tight. Tom's thoughts spun in a sickening whirlpool. He was oblivious to the shouts of the men clearing up the fire debris. He watched them, but he didn't see them. Wherever he looked, his vision was filled with his dead brother's face. His eyes were filled with tears.

So like Jeb, Tom thought, to walk right up to Black Jack and ask him straight.

As morning approached Tom's thoughts steadied. He realized he had no choice. He had to go after the Cheethams. He carefully unbuckled Jeb's gunbelt and slung it over his saddle. He reloaded his Colt and checked the shotgun. He added the remains of Jeb's hardtack to his own and filled his canteen at the spring.

Doc wanted to go with him but Tom insisted on riding out alone. He knew where the Paiute camp was and said he would be able to skirt round it. From there he would be able to find his way to the Cheethams' camp on Honey River. If he dropped down on it through the woods, they wouldn't know he was coming. Doc offered to fetch beads and whiskey from his cabin for Tom to use as trade for a safe passage. Tom wouldn't wait. He said he would take his chances. He just wanted Doc to do one thing and that was to give Jeb a decent burial.

Tom set out in the grey dawn light. Towers of black cloud reared over the mountains above him. The Indian camp was half a day's ride through the woods and Honey River was half a day further. He should be there by nightfall.

Just as he was about to enter the woods above town, Tom looked back at White Fir. He could see Dixie supervising a group of miners stacking chairs and trestles. Frenchie was loading the crates of whiskey back on to a freight wagon. Men were picking their way through the mud and beginning to set up their tents again. Wisps of smoke rose from their campfires. There was no sign of Doc.

Cloud weighed down on the mountain all morning and the sun failed to push through. The air was chill and dew hung on the leaves longer than usual. Tom made good progress, following the route they had taken down the slopes the day before. The track was steep and after a couple of hours he stopped to rest his horse. He dismounted and took a swig of water from his canteen.

He was enclosed in woodland. Valley oaks with their pale-grey bark and their bright spring leaves grew tight together here. Yellow-flowered coffee-berry bushes and thick new clumps of onion grass grew amongst them. There was no wind to move the branches, no sound except for the patter of moisture drops falling from the leaves and the occasional sad call of a mourning dove.

Suddenly, grief for Jeb welled up within Tom. The loneliness of the place made him shiver. He wished he was home. He wished he was anywhere rather than here. He swept the tears from his eyes and fought off the desire to turn back.

Tom's horse pricked up his ears at the sound of a footstep. Tom silently slid his Colt out of its holster and looked round. With the woods this dense, it was almost impossible to tell where the sound was coming from. It got louder. It was too heavy a footstep for a deer, too slow for a man. Some creature was ambling down the track towards him. Tom stood by his horse and covered the track with his Colt.

A packmule pushed its way through the undergrowth, came to an abrupt halt and stared at them. It was loaded high with wooden boxes and canvas bags. A brass tripod was tied on top. Tom holstered his gun. He patted the creature on the muzzle. There was no sign of an owner and a rope trailed from the mule's bridle.

Five minutes later, there was a furious crashing in the undergrowth some way up the track. Someone was trying to run along the path but kept stumbling off into the brush. A second later, a tall young man burst through the screen of branches. He fought to catch his breath.

'Mornin',' he gasped. 'See you got Betsy. Left her to forage while I took a nap and she wandered off. Much obliged to ya for holdin' on to her.'

'Ain't nothin',' Tom said. 'What're you doin' up here? This sure ain't pannin' gear.'

The man laughed. 'I'm a newspaperman. I work for the *California Daily Star* outa Sacramento.' He held out his hand. 'Virgil B. Flute.'

Tom shook his hand. 'Tom Hope. An' what's a newspaperman doin' out here?'

'What newspapermen always do. That's lookin' for stories an' pictures to go with 'em. I take the pictures, then someone else does an engraving from 'em an' they print it in the paper. They sent me out to try an' take pictures of the Paiute. No one ain't done that before, but I bin out on these slopes for three weeks and I ain't seen a soul.'

'If the Paiute don' want you to find 'em, then you don't find 'em. That's what I bin told,' Tom said. 'They're here all right, an' that's fer sure.'

Tom described the visit to the Paiute camp the previous day.

'I was there this morning,' Virgil said. 'Tepees are empty. There's no one there. Everything's been cleared out. Sure looks like they ain't comin' back.'

Tom looked puzzled.

'Anyway, what are you doin' out here? You ain't carryin' no prospectin' gear neither.'

Tom told him about the Cheethams and what had happened to Jeb.

'Hot damn,' Virgil said. 'So you're goin' after 'em by yourself? Mind if I ride along? It would be a big story for me. I might be able to get some pictures too. If I got a picture of the Cheetham Gang, that story would be on every front page from here to Boston. 'Sides that, it'd be company. I been goin' plumb crazy on my own. Another day out here an' I'll be talkin' to the squirrels. That's why I was headed back.'

Tom reflected, 'Can't hurt none. Can't travel faster than a mule through these woods anyhow.'

Virgil beamed. 'If I can get a picture of the Cheetham gang, my editor gonna forgive me an' he might even give me a raise.'

'Forgive you fer what?' Tom said.

'Oh, nothin'.' Virgil looked embarrassed. 'I borrowed some money outa the office payroll an' he caught me, 'fore I could pay it back, 's all. That's how come I got transferred to Sacramento and got this here assignment. No one else in the office would do it. He said it was my last chance. If I didn't come back with some good pictures, I wouldn't be allowed back in the San Francisco office no more.'

'Whatcha borrow the money fer?'

'Met this card player. French fella from Louisiana.

Played a lot with him. Faro, poker, dice games. I won some, he won some. He was waitin' for me, see. Gettin' my confidence. Makin' me think I could beat 'im. Then he took to playin' monte. Now that ain't a hard game, but he took me all right. Cleaned me out of every cent I had, took IOUs until it looked like I was gonna be in hock from here to doomsday. That's when I borrowed the money.'

'What's he look like, this fella?' Tom said.

'Short, skinny. Wears a black jacket. Hangs around with a saloon singer.'

'I know him,' Tom said. 'Name's Frenchie.'

'Well, don't you never play cards with him. Even when you think you're winnin', you're losin'.'

Tom mounted up. 'You gotta horse?'

'Sure have. She's tethered a hundred yards up the track. Left her there while I came lookin' for Betsy.'

The Paiute camp was abandoned just as Virgil had said. There was no sign of a struggle. The Indians had simply packed up everything and left. Tom couldn't help wondering whether it had anything to do with the Cheethams, but he kept the thought to himself. Virgil pointed out the parts of the camp he had photographed.

'When we find them Cheethams,' Tom said, 'they ain't gonna stay still long enough to have their pictures took, less I shoot 'em first. You best keep your camera outa the way till they're !yin' on the ground.'

Tom and Virgil left the Paiute camp just after midday. As the Indians weren't around, they could take a more direct route to Honey River. A path lined with birdsfoot ferns led down the mountainside from here. After riding for an hour, they could see the river below them. Shallow and fast-moving, it was ideal for panning gold.

They stopped at the entrance to a cave. Boulders had been rolled to block it up and other stones jammed between them to seal it. An array of knives, tomahawks and bows had been placed on a ledge above the cave. One of the knives was in good condition but all the other weapons were rusted and rotten. When Virgil picked them up, some of them broke in his hand.

'We shouldn't stay round here,' Tom said, scanning the trees anxiously. 'This here's a Paiute burial cave.'

Virgil jumped down off his horse and began pulling at the stones.

'Don' do that.' Tom said. 'It would take hours to move them stones anyhow. The Paiute block the entrance to the caves real tight to stop animals from gettin' in.'

'I gotta take a picture.' Virgil began unpacking his equipment. 'My editor's gonna love this.'

Virgil set up his camera and arranged the Paiute weapons on the ground in front of the cave, despite Tom's protestations that nothing should be touched. Virgil took three pictures, each from a different angle, then put the weapons back on the ledge. Tom saw him slip a knife into his pocket.

'They catch you with that,' Tom said. 'They're gonna kill you an' you're gonna die slow.'

Virgil laughed. 'Ain't nothin' but a souvenir.'

They reached the river within a couple of hours and began to work their way upstream looking for signs of gold workings. The afternoon sun lit the high slopes to the east with golden light, otherwise the valley was in shadow. The riverbanks were lined with young firs and rabbits played under the trees. They saw squirrels and black-tailed deer, but no sign of human life.

'Cheethams wanted to get as far away from people as they could,' Tom reasoned. 'South woulda taken them nearer to White Fir. Say,' he added, 'I bin thinkin. How come that editor of yours didn't fire you on the spot, when he found out you'd taken the money?'

'Couldn't,' Virgil grinned slyly. 'My pa owns the paper.'

Tom looked at him. 'He owns the *California Daily Star*?'

'Sure,' Virgil said. 'Guess I will too one day. When I do, I'm gonna send that editor up into the Sierras with a mule.' He laughed. 'See how he likes it.'

They found the Cheethams' camp late in the afternoon. Two tents were set up. A circle of burnt grass showed where they had lit a fire. New gold-panning equipment was stacked, unused, in one of the tents. The other was empty. There were no bedrolls, cooking pots, food or anything to suggest that Black Jack and his boys would return soon.

'I don't get it,' Virgil said. 'They come up here to go prospectin' an' they don't even get their feet wet.'

Tom searched the area to see if they had left anything else behind but found nothing. Virgil set his camera up. He took one plate of the deserted camp and then insisted Tom pose in front of the tents for the second shot.

The longer they were there the more certain Tom became that the Cheethams weren't coming back.

'Where d'ya think they've gone?'

'There's plenty of other minin' towns if they're lookin' to steal gold,' Virgil said. 'Hangtown, Gouge Eye. They coulda gone anywhere.'

'I reckon they've headed for Sacramento,' Tom said. 'They're lookin' to spend money right now. That's why they came down to White Fir. They ain't cut out for life up here.'

'I still don't get why they've dragged all this equipment up here an' it ain't used.'

'Who knows?' Tom reflected. 'Argued. Had a fight. They're bad-tempered sonsabitches. Might even have got spooked. Lotta guys do up in the mountains. Guess we better make a camp somewheres up the slope, where we kin keep an eye on this place, and head back to White Fir in the mornin'.'

'This pannin' gear's worth a whole lot,' Virgil suggested. 'The mule's all loaded up. You could take it on your horse.'

Tom spat contemptuously. 'I don't want nothin' o' theirs.'

7

It was mid-morning when Tom and Virgil rode into White Fir. Dixie was standing by the piano singing in the open air. Gracie was serving drinks from the back of the freight wagon. Frenchie was running a dice game at a table close by. A pile of charred canvas and burnt wooden trestles was stacked beside them. The smoke-blackened BON TON SALOON sign was propped against the piano. Tom called a greeting to Dixie as he rode past.

Down the street, the smell of fried onions hung in the air. Zac and another miner, who were sitting at one of the benches, waved Tom over. Virgil ordered himself a plate of liver, onions and baked turnips then, realizing that Tom had no money ordered one for him too.

Tom told Zac about the deserted Indian camp and the Cheethams' abandoned panning gear.

'They never intended to do no prospectin'. Jus' bought the gear so when they came back with your gold they could say they found it up in Honey River. That's my opinion,' Zac said. 'Anyhow those no-good sonsabitches ain't bin back here. Reckon they'll have headed for some cathouse down in Sacramento.'

'That's where I'm headed then,' Tom said grimly. 'I ain't givin' up till I find 'em.'

'Ain't no sign of a bounty hunter,' Zac said. 'Word was put out in Sacramento but nothin' ain't come of it.'

Zac turned to Virgil. 'Ain't you gonna take no pictures of what's happened here?'

'There's been so many fires in the minin' camps, my editor wouldn't be interested,' Virgil said briefly. 'Could take some portraits for the guys to send back home though. Think they'd like that? Would't charge no more 'n' a dollar fifty.'

'I dunno,' Zac said. 'It's gold these guys wanta send back home, not pictures.' Over at the open-air saloon, Dixie finished her song. The few men who were there applauded. Her ginger tomcat was asleep on a chair beside her. She waved to Tom.

'Damn glad the old piana didn't get burnt,' she said. 'We kin carry on so long as we got that.'

There were shouts of delight from Frenchie's dice game. Some of the men were winning. Frenchie looked over at Dixie with a wry smile.

'Won't be too long before their money's in Frenchie's pocket,' Dixie said. 'He'll suggest a game o' faro next.'

'Did that poster get burnt?' Tom asked. 'The one with Jack Cheetham on it?'

'Nope,' Dixie said. 'Still pinned to the pole. Only it's lying on the ground now.'

'Mind if I take it?' Tom said. 'I kin show it around in Sacramento. Might help me track 'em down.'

'Sure. You take it an' welcome.' Dixie said. 'Anythin' to help catch those vermin.'

Tom left Virgil taking portrait photographs of Gracie

and Lisa May for a dollar each and the promise of a dance. He fed and watered his horse in preparation for the ride down to Sacramento. Just as he was about to leave, a Pony Express rider galloped in to town, kicking up a storm of mud. The rider leapt off his horse and dashed up the steps to the office. Moments later, Willy, the clerk, appeared at the doorway in his shirtsleeves and eyeshade, waving a copy of the *California Daily Star*.

'Injun attack!' Willy yelled. 'Wagon train attacked east o' Lake Tahoe.'

A crowd gathered quickly. The Pony Express clerk read aloud from the *Daily Star*.

> A band of Paiute Indians, who have previously lived peacefully in the eastern Sierra, went on the rampage and attacked a wagon train on the high ground between the Walker River and Lake Tahoe. Thirty-eight were killed including women and children out of a total of fifty-three settlers. The attack came as a complete surprise.
>
> One survivor, Mrs Ellen Garrety, wife of Rev. Thomas Garrety, who was killed in the attack, said that her husband and some of the settlers had come across a group of Paiute women and their children the previous day at a tributary to the Walker River. In her opinion, the attack can be viewed as revenge for the treatment of these women by the settlers.
>
> Riders have been sent to alert the military at Fort Grapevine and Fort Plymouth but at the time of going to press, no response has yet been received.

Zac's voice was heard above the murmurings of the crowd.

'We just do what we used to do years ago, when the Injuns were riled. If you're leavin' White Fir an' goin' east into the mountains, you let someone from the Miners' Committee know where you're goin' and when you're leavin'. Then you tell 'em when you get back. That's 'bout all we kin do.'

The crowd drifted away. Zac came over to Tom.

'Damn incomers,' he said. 'They don' understand that if you come across the Paiute, you gotta keep real quiet an' back away. You don't do nothin' to them, they won't do nothin' to you. Doc Morgan is the only person I ever knowed who can get along with 'em. That's because he learned their language. An' he's real careful when he's around 'em, I seed 'im. You hear any more about this when you're down in Sacramento, you be sure to let us know.'

Tom mounted up. He ran his hand over the folded Wanted poster in his pants pocket, just to check that it was there.

A few miles down the track he met a lone rider heading in the direction of White Fir. He wore a dusty plainsman's hat and a buckskin shirt. Twin Colts hung in his gunbelt. Tom asked if he had heard about the attack at Lake Tahoe. The man said he had but that there was no danger this far east. He wouldn't say what his business was in White Fir, so Tom knew at once that he was a bounty hunter. The man did not ask for information or invite confidence. Tom held back from telling him what he knew about the Cheethams. Only too well, he remembered Jeb saying that there was nothing to stop any bounty hunter from pocketing their gold if he caught up with them.

*

It was a two-day ride from White Fir to Sacramento. Late the following afternoon, Tom could see Sacramento spread out on the plain ahead of him. Straight streets of two-storey wooden houses ran down to the river. A forest of the masts of snagboats and packets together with the narrow funnels of the San Francisco riverboats lined Front Street Quay. Even from here, Tom could make out the activity of the place.

Piles of goods, unloaded on the dockside, stood ready for transportation; wagons and carts moved up and down the streets; smoke from ovens drifted up into the pale sky.

Down on the plain, the air lost its mountain chill. Tom pulled his hat down over his eyes against the bright sunlight. The warm air lifted his spirits although the purpose of his journey remained a cold stone in his heart. He took off his jacket as he rode along. A wagon laden with mining equipment passed him, heading for the goldfields. In the mountain settlements, where payments were made in gold, traders could increase their profits tenfold on even the simplest tools.

Tom had only two ways of raising money. He could find work on the docks or he could sell Jeb's gun. He headed down the long street to the waterfront. The nearer he got, the more the air was filled with the sour, salty smell of the river. Tom left his horse at a livery stable on the corner. He gave the owner twenty cents for a feed, water and brush-down.

'Come from the goldfields? Or are ya headed up there?' the owner of the stables said. He sized Tom up with a cynical stare.

'Just come down.'

'Strike it rich?' The man grinned at him through yellow teeth.

'Ain't finished up there yet,' Tom said.

'Gold all ran out in 'forty-nine, I reckon,' the man added. 'More money in runnin' this place, so far as I'm concerned.'

'You might be right,' Tom said.

A river boat was just docking. The huge paddle wheel at its stem beat the water and the tall chimneys belched black smoke. The captain skilfully manoeuvred the bulky vessel alongside the quay so it came to rest with the gentleness of a dancer. Chinese dockworkers made fast the ropes thrown over to them. Passengers jostled along the portside rail, anxious to disembark. More men heading for the mining towns. A gangplank was pushed out from the ship and they filed ashore, excited and anxious at the adventure which lay ahead of them.

Tom pushed his way along the crowded waterfront looking for a shipping-company office where he could ask for work. Eventually, he came to a wooden shack where a pot-bellied clerk sat recording weights and quantities of timber which had been unloaded, in a leather-bound ledger. A man was walking round the yard outside inspecting the piles of timber and calling out the information to him. Tom waited for them to finish.

'You're the third today,' the man said. 'I'm givin' you same answer as I gived the others. This ain't no job fer you. I kin get Chinese fellas to unload the timber fer a dollar a day. They'll work from dawn till night time an' they never complain 'bout nothin'. You stick to minin' or tradin' minin' goods. That's the kinda work you need.'

'I wanta work down on the docks,' Tom said. 'Everyone passes through here sooner or later an' I'm lookin' fer someone.'

The clerk's eyes narrowed. 'Who're you lookin' fer?'

Tom took the Wanted poster out of his pocket and unfolded it. The clerk peered at the picture and read the words carefully. 'Nope,' he said. 'I ain't seen 'im. You a bounty hunter?'

'No, I ain't,' Tom said solemnly. 'He killed my brother. I ain't giving up till I find 'im.'

'Well,' the clerk said, 'I'd like to help ya. But this is a lumber yard. I got a business to run. We don't want no gunfightin' round here. Why don't ya try the gamblin' houses up around China Lake? Seems to me like all the no-good drifters end up there at some time or another.' He looked at Tom coldly and turned back to his ledger.

Tom headed back into the town. The streets were hard, dried mud, rutted with cart tracks. The wooden walls of the buildings were stained dark brown almost up to the top of the ground floor windows, showing the level the floodwaters had reached the last time the river broke through the levees.

Everywhere was busy. Stores, saloons, stable yards and eating houses were all full. Miners loaded new-bought equipment on to carts and mules. Men pushing hand carts, lumbering ox-carts, men on horseback and jostling crowds on foot filled the streets. Everyone was going somewhere and they wanted to be there fast. They had all come to Sacramento for one reason. That was to buy equipment and supplies before heading out for the mining camps. Although the hysteria of 'forty-nine was over, men were still pouring into the Sierras in search of their fortunes.

Turning off J Street on to a narrow thoroughfare, the atmosphere was suddenly different. It was the Chinese quarter. Like J Street, the road was crowded but every one in it was Chinese. The men all wore loose black jackets and pants and had their hair plaited in long queues down their backs. All the store signs were painted in Chinese characters. A man standing outside a doorway caught Tom by the sleeve and beckoned him to come inside.

'Theatre,' the man said cheerfully. 'Canton theatre. Everybody welcome. You come in. You like.'

'Thanks,' Tom said, 'but I. . . .'

The crowd surged and Tom was pushed up the street. He looked back and the man already had someone else by the sleeve, urging them in to see the show.

Not being able to read the shop signs, Tom was unable to tell what most of the buildings were. Occasionally, men standing at doorways would gesture him inside. Tom smiled and waved them away. One open door showed a room full of gaming tables, the players were shouting and slamming their cards down. Piles of money were changing hands. Next door was a laundry. Steam billowed out into the street. There was frantic activity everywhere. Occasionally Tom caught someone's eye. Always, the person would grin at him and speak some greeting he couldn't understand.

At the corner, Tom came to a restaurant. Again, a doorman caught him by the sleeve and pulled him gently towards the entrance. The smell of spiced fish was mouth-watering. He realized he hadn't eaten for two days. Men were sitting on benches eating bowls of rice. Tom held out the last few cents he had in his pocket. A man gestured him to sit and took his money with a nod. Someone moved up to make room for him on the nearest bench. A minute later the man returned with a bowl of rice flavoured with a thin sauce and a few pieces of fish. He handed him a pair of chopsticks. Tom copied the men around him. He held the bowl high and shovelled the rice into his mouth. The dark, salty taste of the sauce was like nothing he had ever tasted before. When he finished the bowl, he could have eaten another straight away. But with his money gone, he was going to have to find work first.

Out on the street again, he left the Chinese quarter and headed back to the riverside. He asked for work at different companies importing goods into Sacramento. They were the nearest depots to the riverboat terminus. Tom figured that sooner or later, the Cheethams would turn up here. The only other way out of the Sierras was over the mountains. At this time of year, while there was spring sunshine down on the plain, many of the mountain passes were still blocked with snow. If they came down out of the goldfields, they would have to come through here.

The foremen at the dockside depots he asked for work viewed him with suspicion. It was odd for a white man to want to work alongside Chinese stevedores. They distrusted him for it, even though Tom was careful not to mention the Cheethams this time. Eventually, he was successful. He came across Sam O'Donnell, the hiring clerk of the riverboat company, sitting outside the quayside shack which served as his office. His left leg was a stump which ended above the knee and was propped for comfort on a tar barrel. A wooden crutch lay across his lap. He told Tom to come back in the morning.

Tom strolled down the length of the quay. The wooden hulls of the boats creaked at their moorings. Dusk was gathering. A lone fisherman sat in his rowboat a little way off shore, his line cast into the grey river. The crowd was drifting back into town now. A few guys were setting out their bedrolls beneath the plane trees that lined the riverbank. They sat smoking and staring reflectively into the water. The loneliness of his situation suddenly came over Tom as he walked back to the livery stable to fetch his own bedroll.

'You kin sleep in here for a quarter,' the owner of the stable called over to him. 'If you ain't got nowhere to go.'

'I'm fine.' Tom waved to him.

The man laughed. 'Ain't got no quarter, neither?' the man jeered. 'Well, you kin go to sleep an' dream of gold, just like the rest of 'em. Nearest you're gonna get, friend.'

Night was falling quickly. Tom climbed into a boatyard, off the main waterfront, and found a sheltered spot between coils of rope and piles of timber where he couldn't be seen. He laid out his bedroll on the hard ground. The gnarled rope dug into his back as he leaned against it. The loneliness of his situation swept over him and his thoughts turned to home. He imagined the Missouri homestead as it had been, in the long summers of his childhood: his father in his old rocker on the porch, smiling down at his boys, even though he had to fight for every breath; Jeb chasing the chickens and making them all laugh; Ruth turning cartwheels round the yard. He wanted so much to write home. But what could he tell them now?

Exhausted, Tom fell into an uneasy sleep broken by men's voices and the sound of water lapping against the quay.

8

A woman's scream tore the night air. Tom sat bolt upright, wide awake. There was the sound of a struggle close by. Men's drunken laughter. Jeering voices. A group of them were on the other side of the pile of timber. Someone fell against the planks, rocking the woodpile above Tom. He grabbed his gun and leapt to his feet.

Round the other side of the stack of timber, three men were attacking a girl. Two of them were holding her arms and the third was leering into her face. The girl was trying to kick herself free. Tom shouted, caught one of the men by the shoulder and wheeled him round. The man stank of whiskey and sweat. Tom shoved his Colt back into his holster and, in one clean movement, brought his fist swinging round to smash against the man's jaw. The man reeled aside, whimpering with pain and surprise.

The girl wrenched herself free from the other two and drove her boot heel hard down on to one of their shins. The man yelped like a puppy. Before any of them had time to go for their guns, Tom's Colt was in his hand again. At the sound of the pistol being cocked, the men cowered behind their hands.

'We weren't doin' nothing, mister,' one of them screamed. 'It's just a Chinese. We was just having some fun is all.'

'Get outa here,' Tom yelled. He waved his gun threateningly. 'Go on. Scat.'

The men scrambled over the fallen planks of wood and disappeared into the night.

Tom holstered his gun. The young woman looked at him fearfully.

'It's OK,' Tom said gently. 'Ain't no one gonna hurt you now.'

'I go,' the young woman said quickly.

'I'll come with you,' Tom said. 'Just in case them guys are still hangin' about.'

The woman ran out of the boatyard, down a dark alley away from the waterfront into the maze of narrow streets which made up Chinatown. The place was closed up. No one was about. The yellow light of oil lamps flickered behind the curtained windows of the gaming houses. Arguing voices could be heard through closed doors.

Someone was standing in the shadows outside a doorway at the end of a street. A tall Chinaman turned towards them. His anxious face broke into smiles as soon as he saw the woman. Then, just as abruptly, his expression turned to anger. He pointed at Tom, continuing his tirade. The woman replied and he began to calm down and listen.

'My sister,' the man said to Tom. 'We owe you a debt. I tell her not to go outside the restaurant. When she does, the men take her.' He mimed picking up someone by their shoulders.

'I am Moshushi,' the man said. He bowed briefly. 'My

sister is Jingzhi.' They smiled at him.

'Tom Hope,' Tom said.

The two conferred briefly together. 'None of the white men like Chinese in California. You the first one who has shown us some kindness. We wish to help you. What can we do?'

'Ain't nothin',' Tom said shyly. 'Anybody woulda done the same.'

'No, no,' Moshushi protested quickly. 'You don't understand what it's like for Chinese people here. You gold miner?'

'I was,' Tom said. 'Right now I'm looking for these guys.' He took the folded poster out of his pocket. 'I'm lookin' for work too.'

Moshushi pushed open the restaurant door and beckoned Tom inside. It was a bare room, filled with hard wooden chairs and tables. He lit an oil lamp and placed it in the centre of a table, smoothed out the poster and stared at it. Eventually, he shook his head.

'No,' he said. 'We don't know these men. White men come into restaurant every night, but not these.' Moshushi looked hard at Tom. 'You say you're looking for work?'

'Yup, sure am.'

'You wanna work for Chinese man?' Moshushi asked cautiously.

'Work's work, ain't it?' Tom said.

'If you want, you can stand by restaurant door in the evening and watch the white men coming in. If there is any trouble, you can put them in the street. I pay one dollar a night and all the food you want.' He grinned at Tom. 'Good offer. This way you can watch out for these men you want to find.'

'Sure is a good offer. I accept.'

'Good,' Moshushi said. 'Start tomorrow night.'

The first grey light of day was seeping into the sky as Tom made his way back to the boatyard. Gulls screeched overhead and the air was chill. Tom collected his bedroll. Chinese dockers were beginning to move about Front Street, in preparation for the new day. Tom made his way to the riverboat company yard, where the clerk had told him to come back. A group of men were already gathered round the office door, waiting for the hiring clerk to arrive.

At 6.30, someone opened the office door from the inside. The clerk stepped out, leaned heavily on his crutch, stuck his thumbs in his belt and appraised the group of waiting men. He noticed Tom and nodded to him.

'All righty,' he said, by way of introduction. 'We got three boats in today. That means I'm gonna need ten extra men. That's extra to the men that was workin' here yesterday.' He spoke slowly, unsure whether he was being understood or not. 'Ten,' he repeated deliberately. 'Comprenday?' He held up ten fingers for everyone to see.

The men looked round at each other. There were twelve of them. The two who had joined the group last, spoke briefly to the others and walked away.

'Well,' the clerk turned to Tom. 'That was easy, weren't it? Usually, they don' understand a damn word I say.'

Within an hour, the first boat had docked. It was a wide decked cargo boat loaded with crates of fruit, vegetables and sacks of flour and rice. Unloading it and stacking the crates on the quay side was back-breaking. The stevedores worked in teams of four, lifting the crates together, manhandling them down the narrow gangplank and stacking them near the entrance to the boat yard. At intervals, wholesalers' wagons rolled up and the men broke off from unloading the boat to heave the crates up on to them while the drivers checked orders and invoices with the shipping company clerk.

The Chinese stevedores were broad-shouldered men with iron muscles. They didn't take a break for three hours. They found their rhythm and worked on through the morning, lifting, carrying, heaving and stacking. They rarely spoke. A look or a gesture told them what they needed to know to get the work done. Mostly, they avoided Tom's gaze, but it was clear that they were surprised that he kept up with the pace they set and they respected him for it.

When, at last, the decks of the cargo boat were empty, the men sat on the ground, leaning against the wooden wall of the company office and passed a tin mug of water between them. Tom accepted the drink gratefully. The day was bright. The sun had climbed in the sky and a river breeze cooled them.

They watched the empty boat get up steam until black smoke belched from its narrow funnel. The skipper called out a brief command and one of the crewmen hauled in the gangplank. Sam emerged from his office and nodded to the Chinaman sitting nearest the door. The man immediately stood up, walked over to the mooring ropes and unhitched them. They slapped on to the surface of the water. The skipper waved briefly to Sam and the boat began to turn out into the river.

Sam indicated that Tom should follow him into the office. Inside, Tom blinked, letting his eyes adjust to the shadows. Ledgers were open on a desk and a pile of invoices were impaled on a metal spike.

'Ain't no need fer you to sit out there with them,' the clerk said, scratching his round belly. 'Want some coffee?' He indicated a pot bubbling on a small iron stove.

'You gonna give some to the other guys?' Tom asked.

The clerk glanced at him suspiciously. 'You kin ask 'em, I guess. It'll be deducted off their pay. They won't want it anyhow. They don't like the taste of it.'

Tom stepped outside. 'Coffee?' he said and mimed pouring into a cup. The men looked up at him and grinned. They shook their heads and raised their cups of water. They broke into fast conversation as Tom stepped back inside.

'What did I tell ya?' the clerk said. He sat down at his desk.

Tom took a tin mug off a shelf and poured himself a cup of coffee.

'Much obliged,' he said.

'Sure is nice to have someone to speak some English to,' Sam said. 'Them Chinese fellas. Damn good workers, most of 'em. But they don't speak no English.' He chuckled at his own remark. 'Anyhow, why ain't you up in the hills diggin' for gold?'

'I was,' Tom said. 'I had a claim. But it didn't work out.'

'They reckon that come next year, there'll be more miners leavin' the Sierras than comin' in. Gold's runnin' out now.'

'Could be,' Tom said.

'Four years ago, I was crewin' on the Josephine, a passenger boat outa New York City. Brung fellas all crazy fer gold. Sailed round the Cape right to San Francisco.

Helluva voyage. Took a hundred and thirty-seven days.'

'Yeah?' Tom said.

'Damnedest thing.' Sam looked out into the sunlight. 'Soon as we got to San Francisco, the passengers disembarked and the crew did too. And the captain. Whole lotta them. Just abandoned the ship right there in San Francisco harbour an' headed off for the goldfields. Every one of 'em was convinced they was gonna strike it rich. Never saw hide nor hair of any of 'em since. Turned out that they'd all listened to the stories the passengers told on the voyage and reckoned gold was there for the takin'. Wouldn't let me go along on accounta my leg. So I got work with the riverboat company an' ended up here.'

'I heard stories like that before,' Tom said.

'We weren't the first,' Sam said, 'No sir. San Francisco harbour was full of abandoned boats. Tell ya what, though, I seen guys spend years in the goldfields an' come away with nothin' but the clothes they stand up in.'

'Yeah,' Tom said. He got up, as if he had been reminded of something. 'Look, I'm kinda keeping an eye out for someone. I'm gonna take a walk up the quay.'

Sam nodded. 'OK. Next boat should be in inside of half an hour.'

Front Street Quay was alive. Teams of Chinese dockers were unloading barges. Horse-drawn wagons and lumbering ox-carts, piled with provisions and mining equipment, edged past each other. Horseback riders and pedestrians threaded in and out of the crowd. Cigar-smoking wholesalers scoured the piles of goods on the dockside for their orders. Riverboat captains directed the unloading from the vantage point of their bridges. A man was working his way down the line of plane trees, nailing up posters which advertised a newly opened Miners' Variety Store. Groups of exhausted men, miners returning home, sat beneath the trees waiting for a passage down river.

Tom took the Wanted poster from his pocket and folded it so that only the picture was visible. He showed it to some of the men beneath the plane trees and then began stopping passers-by. No one recognized the Cheethams.

Once again, the loneliness of his situation started to overcome him. Out of nowhere, grief for Jeb tore at him from inside. He turned and strode back to the riverboat company quay, where a great paddleboat was just docking. Sam was shouting orders and the Chinese shoremen were getting to their feet. A sailor leapt off the boat and made it fast at the stern, then walked up to the bow. He pulled a gangplank out on to the dockside. The anxious, excited miners filed ashore, failing to notice the groups of tired, dispirited men watching them from beneath the plane trees.

By evening, when the third boat had been unloaded, Tom's whole body ached. His shoulders and back burned with pain. Sam paid him, along with the rest of the men and told them all to come back in the morning. He asked Tom to stay on for company through the evening. Tom turned him down and, not wanting to say too much, told him he had to meet someone in the town. He made his way through the maze of streets to the restaurant where Jingzhi was pleased to see him.

9

Tom spent his evenings leaning against the door frame of the restaurant. There was never much trouble. He directed all the drunks to the cathouse across the street. The white guys who came to the restaurant were either tired miners, back from the goldfields, or new arrivals just off the riverboat. Either way, none of them had much money and the place was mostly quiet.

From time to time, arguments broke out when someone hadn't understood what they had ordered or hadn't understood that the only food on the menu was rice and fish. Tom noticed how although the miners were quite willing to save their money by using the restaurant, they treated Moshushi and Jingzhi with contempt. But Moshushi, who did most of the serving, continued to smile and avoid catching the customer's eye as insults rained down on him. The men assumed that he couldn't understand them.

Tom began showing the picture of Cheetham to the customers as they entered the restaurant. Occasionally, someone had heard of the Cheetham Gang, but no one recognized them. On the third night, he pinned up the poster at eye-level, by the door. Men glanced at it as they entered, but again no one knew the Cheethams. Tom began by taking the poster down at the end of the evening and keeping it with him. But, after a few days, he got so used to it being there, that he sometimes forgot and it stayed, pinned up and unremarked on, by the door.

Working on the docks by day and watching the restaurant door in the evenings became a regular routine for Tom. Sam, the river boat company clerk, was always pleased to have someone to talk to, and put him in charge of a gang of workers. Moshushi appreciated him sorting out arguments at the restaurant and keeping troublemakers away. His team of dockers liked him and he got to know the regulars at the restaurant. Jingzhi gave him all the food he could eat and all the green tea he could drink. He had no need to spend any money and was able to save his pay. Moshushi even found a straw mattress for him and he slept in the restaurant after it closed.

Tom regularly checked on his horse down at the livery stable. The owner was content to look after the creature, provided he was paid. For a few cents a day extra, he found someone to exercise her.

One evening, Tom was late arriving at the restaurant. Two of his usual team hadn't turned up for work at the quay and it had fallen to Tom and the others to do their share of the work. Then there had been an argument because the men had demanded extra pay and Sam insisted that he would only pay the same daily rate per man, whether there was a full team or not. Eventually Tom intervened and managed to persuade Sam to compromise. He agreed to pay one man's money, on top of the wages, to be divided between the others.

When Tom arrived at the restaurant, he immediately saw that the Wanted poster had been torn down. It was screwed up on the ground. Tom picked it up and smoothed it flat again. He pushed open the door a couple of inches. He could see Heck and Buck Cheetham inside, sitting at a table facing the door.

Tom heard the sound of a gun being cocked close to his ear. He froze. Then he heard a voice whisper 'You stand real still, mister. An' you stay real quiet.' He felt the heat of a man's breath against his neck. Someone removed his gun from its holster and shoved Tom against the wall. He felt the hard barrel of a gun pressed up against his temple.

'Now you turn round real slow, an' you tell me what you're doin'.'

Tom turned slowly, expecting to see Black Jack Cheetham's leering face. But it wasn't him. The man had a half-moon scar under one eye and looked hard at Tom. He pressed the barrel of his pistol against the side of Tom's head.

Tom knew the man from somewhere, but he couldn't place him.

The man produced a pair of handcuffs from his pocket, while keeping the barrel of his gun against Tom's head.

'Now, you just put these bracelets on an' you remember that I kin blow your brains out as easy as spit.'

'I ain't with them,' Tom protested.

'No? Then what're you doin' here?'

The man slid the barrel of his gun round the side of Tom's face until it jabbed him under his chin.

'Jus' shaddup. I ain't takin' no chances on you.' He shoved the handcuffs into Tom's hand.

Tom cuffed himself. The man locked the cuffs and slipped the key into his pocket. He pushed Tom to one side, opened the door and stepped into the restaurant.

Heck went for his gun the moment the door opened. He kicked the table over, spat out a mouthful of rice and leapt to one side, firing wildly in the direction of the door. The stranger emptied four shots into him and then turned to Buck and shot him twice in the chest. Buck didn't even have time to draw his weapon.

The restaurant exploded. Men dived for cover. Plates, cups, food and furniture went flying. An oil lamp was knocked over and a pool of burning oil spread across the floor. Jingzhi, who had been carrying a pile of crockery out to the kitchen, screamed in terror at the sound of the shots, and threw the plates up into the air so that they rained down over everyone and smashed on the floor. Moshushi burst through the kitchen door with a pile of cloths, threw them over the pool of flame and began stamping on them hysterically, beating out the fire. Tom, still handcuffed, ran in through the door and began to help him.

Men picked themselves up off the floor and dashed for the door. The Cheetham boys lay in pools of blood. Heck was still, face down beside the wall. Buck lay sobbing weakly.

The gunman turned to Tom, as he pushed new shells into the chamber of his Colt.

'Now, you were gonna tell me what you're doin' here.'

'He work for me,' Moshushi burst out. 'He stop the drunks coming in. He good man.'

The gunman snorted. 'Well, he didn't stop these two

animals gettin' in.'

He reached in his pocket for the key to the handcuffs and gave it to Tom.

'You're the bounty hunter, I guess,' Tom said.

'S'right,' the man said. 'Dan Lynchburg, outa Texas. But I ain't seen home now fer some time. I bin on the trail of these Cheethams for a coupla months. Got word they was up at White Fir.'

Tom remembered where he had seen the man. It was up on the road out of White Fir, the day he left for Sacramento.

The burning oil lamp was put out now. Moshushi began setting the tables and chairs upright again and Jingzhi brought a broom in from the kitchen and began sweeping up the carpet of wasted rice and smashed plates. They ignored the white men talking at one end of the room and the broken, bloody bodies at the other. Buck started groaning again.

Lynchburg strode over to Buck and nudged him with the toe of his boot. 'Dead or alive, son. Don't make no difference to me. Soon's morning comes I'm gonna get someone from the Wells Fargo Bank to identify you, so's I kin claim my *re*-ward.'

'Pa?' Buck was delirious. 'I bin shot, Pa. I knowed they'd catch up with us. I told you they would but you wouldn't listen.'

'Yeah,' Lynchburg sneered. 'An' you know where your pa is now? He's right where I left him, cuffed to a wagon up in White Fir with that fella from the Miners' Committee standin' guard on him.'

'Pa?' Buck continued. 'You changed when Ma died. It made you mean. You wouldn'ta done all this if Ma had bin alive. We woulda stayed back in Kansas on the farm. We never woulda gone theivin' like we done.' He paused. 'I'm thirsty, Pa.'

Jingzhi put down her broom and went to the kitchen to fetch him a mug of water. By the time she came back, Buck was dead.

Lynchburg nodded to Moshushi. 'Soon's I git the reward money, I'll pay forty dollars for your trouble.' He shook his head. 'Fellas like them never learn. I point a gun at 'em an' the first thing they do is start shootin'. They don' think no one's faster than them.'

A crowd had gathered outside. Girls leaned out of the windows of the cathouse across the street. Everyone's face was tight with worry. There was often trouble in Chinatown. Moshushi explained what had happened and the crowd seemed relieved. It was someone else's fight this time.

'Could you cook me up some o' that rice an' fish, you was servin' earlier?' Lynchburg asked Jingzhi. 'I'm always hungry after a shootin'.'

He sat down at a corner table.

Moshushi said 'You pay a hundred dollar. Forty for breakages, sixty because restaurant customers won't come in with bodies here.'

Lynchburg looked at him coldly. 'Sixty.'

'Eighty dollar,' Moshushi insisted. 'Customer don't come, so you must pay instead.'

Lynchburg considered. 'Alright then, eighty. An' I don't pay for the meal.'

'Agree,' Moshushi said. 'You take bodies away in the morning. Soon.'

Tom and Lynchburg dozed in chairs by the door for the rest of the night. Early next morning, when the streets began to fill with people, Lynchburg left for the Wells Fargo Bank to get someone to formally identify the Cheethams.

Tom was alone in the restaurant when Lynchburg left. Moshushi had gone to the fish market and Jingzhi was cleaning the kitchen. Tom checked Heck and Buck's pockets for the leather purse which contained the gold. He knew it was a long shot. It was unlikely that Black Jack would have parted with it, even to his sons. Anyway, their pockets were empty. There were two horses which had been tethered outside all night. Tom slipped out and checked the saddle-bags and bedrolls. Again nothing.

There was no money either. Nothing to suggest the Cheetham boys had turned the gold into dollar bills. Tom reasoned that there was a good chance Black Jack still had the nuggets, or, if he didn't, that the gold was still somewhere in White Fir.

Lynchburg came back sometime later accompanied by the manager of the Wells Fargo Bank, a tall, slow-speaking man who took off his hat when he entered the restaurant, revealing a mane of curly grey hair. An undertaker came with them. He wore a greasy tail coat, skipped lightly over the bodies and took the measurements without waiting to be asked. The Wells Fargo man briefly glanced at the faces of the two corpses. His lip curled with contempt as he made a positive identification.

'Good work, Mr Lynchburg,' he said gravely. 'Now, when you bring in Black Jack Cheetham, we kin issue the reward.'

'I'm gonna need some money on account,' Lynchburg protested.

'The reward is for the whole Cheetham gang. It would

be against bank policy to pay out for a part-completed job, now wouldn't it?'

'You know I can't get to White Fir now. Butterfield ain't sent no mail coaches up there since the first attack. That's nigh on two weeks ago.'

'I ain't heard about no attack,' Tom said.

'Well, you wanna keep your ears open. There's Paiute raiding parties up there right now. There was some trouble with a wagon train over by Lake Tahoe. Injuns blamed the settlers as usual. Nex' thing you know, there's raiding parties an' braves all fired up an' on the warpath. Butterfield won't risk goin' up there. No one won't risk it. I pity the poor souls up there. For all we know there mightn't be none of 'em left alive.'

'Well, all that's as maybe,' the Wells Fargo Manager said. 'Point is, we ain't payin' out no *re*-ward on a job that ain't finished. Company policy.' He considered. 'Best thing you kin do, Mr Lynchburg, if you'll take my advice, is to wait until the Paiute have calmed down, then get on up to White Fir. If that good-fer-nothin' Jack Cheetham is still alive, drill a couple 'o holes in 'im and bring him back down to civilization. That way you'll get your reward.'

'You left Cheetham in the charge of Zac Johnson, didn't you?' Tom said.

'Sure did,' Lynchburg said grimly. 'Shoulda shot 'im right there 'n then.'

Moshushi arrived with a sack of fish and armfuls of vegetables.

'It's all right,' Lynchburg said. 'Undertaker's gonna take 'em away right now.'

'I should be down at the quay,' Tom said.

Outside, Tom unhitched one of the Cheethams' horses and mounted up. A shotgun was tied on one side of the saddle He tugged the reins and rode up the street in the direction of the road to White Fir.

10

Tom lay on a rocky ridge looking down over White Fir. He had left the Sacramento road a mile back, tethered his horse in a spinney and made his way up through the woods on foot.

The town was a ruin. Main Street was empty and still. The wagon selling red-eye had gone; the piano was tipped over in the mud and the tables outside the food tent were overturned. The charred remains of the saloon tent was in an untidy heap, other tents were spread over the ground like rags. A wagon lay on its side outside the Pony Express office. A buzzard was pecking at the carcass of a squirrel on the ground beside it.

Lying there, Tom began to notice small details. A woman's shoe lay in the street beside the overturned wagon. There was a pile of what looked like flour on the porch outside the Pony Express office. The door to the hardware store was half-off its hinges. Tom puzzled over this and checked that his Colt was fully loaded.

As he watched, the buzzard which had been pecking at the animal carcass suddenly pounded up into the air. Tom lay still. A minute later a young Paiute brave, hardly more than a boy, appeared from round the far side of the Pony Express office, carrying a stack of dry brushwood. He bent low, out of sight of the windows, left the brushwood heaped against the door and slipped around the back of the building again. A few minutes later another youth appeared and silently placed a second pile of kindling against the first. Tom watched, trying to figure out where the rest of the raiding party was.

This process continued, on and off, for an hour until brushwood was piled right across the front of the building. Tom couldn't make out any other Paiute braves. He couldn't tell who was inside the Pony Express office either. He had a Colt .45 and a belt almost full of shells. Of course, the Paiute could have found his horse by now and could know he was there. He looked around him anxiously. His stomach felt as if he had just swallowed a mugful of sour milk.

Someone called out in Paiute language. It was a man's voice. The words, harsh-sounding and unfamiliar, echoed round the valley. There was silence. Then the voice called again. Tom strained to hear where the speaker was, but the woods and the echo hid him. He seemed to be demanding something, or threatening something, maybe.

As Tom watched, a burning arrow was fired from the woods over to his left. It arced high and fell steeply, lodging in the ground a few yards in front of the door of the Pony Express office. Tom watched flames lick up the shaft of the arrow until it burned itself out.

The voice called again. It sounded mocking this time. There was a pause, then someone answered from inside the Pony Express office. It was Doc. He called out in Paiute, clearly and lightly. The tone of his reply sounded calm and reasonable, like the day when they had met the brave near the Paiute camp.

There was no reply from the woods this time. But after a few minutes, a second burning arrow raced high into the sky and plummeted into the ground a yard closer to the office door than the first. The flames began to consume it again, a casual, terrifying threat. A minute later, the Express office door was pushed open, shoving aside the pile of brushwood. Doc strode determinedly out carrying a canteen. He walked briskly over to the burning arrow, appearing not to hurry, and upended the canteen over it. The shaft of the arrow was left charred and smoking in a pool of water. Doc turned and strode quickly back into the office and pulled the door to.

Tom waited. Then he counted ten burning arrows, on a high arc, landing still closer to the office than before. Tom wondered who was in the building with Doc, or whether anyone was. He considered his options. If he tried to run down into the building to join Doc, he would almost certainly get an arrow in his back before he made it to the door. If he tried to fetch help from Sacramento he wouldn't be back for two days.

The Paiute raiding party were still enjoying threatening Doc for the moment. When they lost patience, they would set fire to the building and move in for the kill. They were clearly in no hurry to do this yet. This stand-off could go on for days, the Paiute could be waiting for nightfall or, Tom knew well, the attack could come within the next half-hour.

Terrified in case the Paiute had spotted him, Tom wriggled backwards off the rock. He kept his eye on the Pony Express office for as long as he could, then he turned and picked his way back through the undergrowth to where he had left his horse. He was relieved to find her still tethered to a dogwood, where he had left her. He found a handful of shotgun shells in the saddle-bag and shoved them into his pocket. Now and then he stayed still and listened, straining to catch any sound which might tell him where the Paiute were. He heard nothing.

He untied the horse and led her carefully back through the undergrowth to the road. Although he was more exposed here, he figured that the Paiute would want to stay hidden in the woods and would keep away from the road. He began to walk his horse the two miles up to White Fir, his eyes desperately scanning the undergrowth beside the track.

At the bend in the road where the Cheethams had robbed the stage, Tom turned his horse into the woods. After pushing a hundred yards or so into the brush, well out of sight of the road, he dismounted and untied the shotgun from the saddle. He picked his way on foot, as silently as he could, through the undergrowth and up the slope which would take him round the back of the buildings.

It was slow going. Fear crawled around in Tom's stomach like a spider. He paused every few steps to listen and look around him. Once, he heard the mocking Paiute voice echoing round the valley again and then Doc's singsong in reply. As long as they were talking, he thought, the people in the Pony Express office were safe.

Tom reached the flat rock at the top of the slope above the settlement. The woods thinned out here and he could see over the valley. At the edge of the brush on the opposite slope a group of Paiute braves were gathered round a small fire. Their ponies stood quietly a little way off. Some of the braves were sitting on the ground, others were slumped against tree trunks, talking and laughing together. Tom could clearly see empty liquor bottles on the ground beside them. Every few minutes, one of the braves would hold an arrow in the fire until it was alight. Then, barely pausing to take aim, he shot it in a high trajectory so that it came down precisely, a few yards short of the brushwood piled against the front of the Pony Express office.

Tom froze. There was a movement in the brush immediately below him. A scrabbling noise followed the sound of someone pushing through the saplings. A minute later, a young black-tailed deer appeared between the trees. It picked its way cautiously over the uneven ground and then hesitated, catching Tom's scent. Another disturbance in the thicket behind it made it spring away into the woods again. A young Paiute brave appeared, holding his bow ready, the arrow slotted in place. He stared hard into the undergrowth, raised the bow to his shoulder and then lowered it again, still staring down the path the deer had taken. Tom recognized him as one of the boys who had been piling brushwood round the Pony Express office.

Something touched the back of Tom's neck. He reached behind him to brush away an insect. The back of his hand grazed against something sharp. He turned. The second young brave was standing over him with bow pulled back and the arrow tip inches from Tom's head. Tom ducked aside and kicked the boy's legs from under him. He tumbled forwards. The arrow glanced against the rock. The brave dropped the bow, in an effort to save himself from falling. Tom held up his arms to stop the

Paiute landing on top of him.

Below them, the brave who had been tracking the deer loosed off an arrow which went wide over their heads. The brave reached for his hunting-knife, Tom held his wrist with one hand and shoved his Colt against the boy's chest. Tom didn't fire. The Paiute seemed scarcely more than fifteen. He pulled away from Tom, unafraid of the gun and grabbed the knife out of his belt. Tom tried to get to his feet and heard the sound of a second arrow, fired from below, slice through the air. It passed over Tom's shoulder and caught the boy in the chest. He fell back. Tom heard the brave who had fired crashing downhill through the undergrowth.

The boy's body lay on the flat rock. Blood welled from where the arrow lodged in him. Tom grabbed the shotgun and leaped down off the rock in pursuit of the brave. He could hear him tearing into the undergrowth ahead of him. He caught sight of him, dodging quickly through the trees. He saw him glance back at Tom. Branches and saplings whipped across Tom's face as he ran tumbling and stumbling downhill, trying to keep the brave within sight. He saw him leap over a fallen tree trunk, turn and drop to one knee.

Horrified, Tom saw that the brave already had his bow in his hand and was reaching over his shoulder for an arrow. Hurtling fast downhill, unable to stop, Tom was careering right into the brave's line of fire. The brave drew back the bowstring. Tom raised the scattergun as he ran and pulled both triggers. The shot echoed round the valley like a thunderclap. The brave leaped backwards in a grotesque somersault, his arrow was loosed wildly into bushes. Tom threw himself on to the ground.

The echo of the shot died and the whole valley was

filled with silence. Nothing moved. Tom gingerly picked himself up. The twisted body of the young brave lay a few yards away. He had broken his neck.

Tom grabbed the scattergun, stepped around the body and continued down through the woods. At the bottom of the slope, he waited amidst the trees looking for signs of life. He was only a few yards away from the back wall of the Pony Express office here. Brushwood was stacked against it. The Paiute braves had clearly finished piling kindling against the back and had been starting round the front when they were distracted by the deer. The pile of bone-dry brushwood had turned the Pony Express office into a tinder box. One flaming arrow and the place would be ablaze.

Out of sight of the braves on the other side of the valley, Tom began to pull down the pile of brushwood and throw the dry branches into the undergrowth. When he had finished, he peeked round the side of the building. There was no brushwood here. The Paiute had been planning to set light to the front and back. There were no doors or windows in the side walls.

Banking on the fact that at least some of the Paiute braves would have skirted round the valley, to find out what had happened to the boys, Tom decided to head round the front of the building. He pushed two shells into the breech of the scattergun and, treading softly, kept close to the wall. At the far end, he peered out into the street.

The stumps of burned out arrows were dotted in the mud in front of the Express office like a row of blackened teeth. The braves had managed to pile brushwood the length of the wall, right across the door, up to the level of the windows, without being seen from inside. There was no movement from across the valley. Tom waited. The buzzard landed again, its great wings pounding the air, and began pecking at what Tom had first thought was a dead squirrel in the middle of the street, beside the overturned wagon. Now he saw it was a severed human arm.

Tom waited. Still no sound from the other side of the valley. He wondered if the braves had heard him moving the brushwood. Maybe they had left. Maybe the shot had scared them. The longer Tom stood there, the more confident he became. He wanted to call out to find out who was inside the building, but stopped himself in case the braves could hear him, wherever they were. After half an hour of crouching in the dirt at the side of the office, with occasional nervous glances over his shoulder to check that no one was coming for him from behind, Tom couldn't wait any longer.

He stepped round the front of the building and began tearing down the pile of brushwood. He threw it out into the street. He had worked his way along one side and almost reached the door, when a flaming arrow landed amongst the branches on the other side of the door. Tom did not stop. He continued faster now, grabbing the wood and throwing it out into the street with one hand while clutching the shotgun with the other. Another arrow landed in the brushwood. Then another. The wood spat and crackled as flames danced through the branches.

The office door burst open. It was Doc. He joined in with Tom, seizing burning branches and heaving them away from the building. A stream of arrows followed. It was soon done. The branches were burning themselves out in the middle of the street. Tom and Doc wrenched the door open and hurled themselves inside as another arrow hit the woodwork.

11

Tom and Doc picked themselves up off the wooden floor. They heard the soft thudding as a succession of arrows bit into the front wall of the building.

'Why, if it ain't young Tom Hope.' Dixie's voice was as dry as chalk. 'I sure as hell hope you've got the cavalry with ya.'

Tom blinked to let his eyes adjust to the shadows inside. The office was smaller than he had thought. Flour sacks were propped all across the length of the front wall beneath the windows. Dixie, Virgil and the girls were leaning against them, keeping low, out of the line of the windows. They were white-faced and terrified. Frenchie shoved the oak counter back across the door.

Dixie held a pistol in one hand; her other arm was around Gracie's shoulders. Frenchie was beside them. Beneath the window on the other side of the door, Virgil and Lisa May were huddled together. At the side of the room, Zac sat beside Black Jack Cheetham, whose wrists were locked together in handcuffs.

Tom told them all briefly about the brushwood piled at the back of the building and about the young Paiute boys.

'They were plannin' on burnin' us out, back an' front?' Dixie said.

'I ain't so sure,' Doc said. 'I think this is just a bunch o' young bucks liquored up an' out on a spree. They're sportin' with us. All this shootin' burnin' arrows short of the buildin'. They're enjoyin' themselves.'

'Don't mean they ain't plannin' to kill us all in the end,' Gracie said tearfully. She turned and buried her head in Dixie's shoulder.

'Look,' Doc continued, 'they coulda killed us all by now if they'da wanted to. They're 'fraid to, is what I reckon.'

'That's a nice idea, Doc,' Zac said. 'But I don't buy it. What about what they asked you for? Ain't they waitin' for us to go along with it?'

'What did they ask fer?' Tom said.

Doc looked worried. 'It ain't serious. They're jus' playin' with us.'

'Tell 'im, Doc,' Dixie said coldly.

Doc sighed. 'They want us to send the girls out. They say if we do that, they'll let the rest of us go.' He stared at the floor. 'If we don't, they'll kill us and take them anyway.'

Silence hung in the air like a fog, deadening their ability to think.

'Just you all be sure o' this,' Dixie said. 'If anyone o' you fine gentlemen even thinks o' savin' his own skin by sendin' any one o' my girls out there, or me for that matter, then the first shot I fire with this here pistol will blow his pecker off. The second will be for any damn Injun who comes near us.'

She pointed her pistol at each of the men in turn. 'That's a promise.'

'You ain't gotta worry, Dix,' Frenchie said. 'These boys all know these Injuns ain't in the mood to trade nothin'. If they got a mind to kill us, that's what they'll do.' He turned to Tom. 'You tol' the army what's goin' on up here?'

'I ain't,' Tom said. 'But they'll know soon enough if they don't already. Whole o' Sacramento knows an' Butterfield has cancelled sending the stage up by this route.'

'We just gotta wait it out then,' Frenchie said.

'Gotta get organized,' Zac said. 'We need to make an inventory of what food and water we got, 'case we're here for a while. Then we need to start a rota so we don't all fall asleep at the same time.'

Black Jack spoke for the first time. 'What about you, mister?' he said to Tom. 'What are you doin' back here?'

'I got some unfinished business,' Tom said cautiously. 'I saw what was goin' on an' came in to lend a hand.'

'That's mighty generous of you,' Black Jack's voice was bitter with sarcasm. 'Looks like everyone's business gonna finish pretty soon, don' it?'

Tom changed the subject. 'Where's everyone else? I ain't seen another soul outside this buildin'.'

'They took off up to their claims,' Frenchie said. 'Soon as they heard the Injuns might be comin'. They reckoned they'd be safe if they jus' scattered an' hid themselves away. None of us ain't got claims to hide in, so when we realized the Butterfield wasn't gonna come, we jus' loaded up a wagon ready to head down to Sacramento. That was when the Paiute rode through, whoopin' an' yellin'. They tipped over the wagon. We skedaddled in here. That was two days ago.'

'You bin in here two days?' Tom said, incredulous.

'Tell 'im about yesterday,' Lisa May said.

No one spoke. Tom looked from face to face but no one caught his eye.

'We don' wanna be talkin' about that right now,' Doc said sharply. 'Zac's right. We gotta make a list of what stores we got. How much water.' He turned to Tom. 'One of us has bin sneakin' out at night to fill the canteens from the spring.'

'Stores is all out back, if someone kin fin' the courage to go out there an' check,' Frenchie said. 'There ain't much left, I'm tellin ya. We ate too much on the first day. Maybe one of us could get across the street to the hardware store. Boun' to be supplies in there. Might fin' some ammo too.'

The Paiute called from somewhere across the valley. His voice sounded full of mocking questions. Everyone in the Express office looked at Doc.

'Well?' Dixie said.

Doc looked grave. 'He says one of us has killed two of their young braves.'

'What else?' Tom said. 'He said more 'n that.'

'He wants us to send a woman out for each of the dead braves.' Doc's words caught in his throat. Then he added 'Right now. He says we kin have 'em back in an hour.'

'Or what?'

'Didn't say nothin' else. 'Cept that one of the boys was his son.'

Gracie clung to Dixie and sobbed. Dixie cocked her pistol, laid it down in her lap and stared angrily at the men. Lisa May moved closer to Virgil.

Silence hung in the air for a moment, then Black Jack

laughed. 'Seems to me like that's the best offer we had all day. Now which o' you pretty little saloon doves is gonna step up an' save us?'

'You hobble that fat lip o' yours,' Dixie spat. 'We don' wanna hear none o' your vile ideas.'

'I'm just sayin',' Black Jack went on with false reasonableness, 'if the girls went out there, that would buy us some time. We could slip out an' into the woods while them Injuns was all occupied.'

'I'm warnin' you,' Dixie said. She waved the Colt at him. 'I could blow your brains out as easy as laughin'. You jus' shut your flapper an' keep it shut or I'll do jus' that.'

'This is bullshit,' Frenchie said. 'I'm goin' out back to check over the supplies, if no one else'll do it.'

The others sat in grim silence. The Paiute brave started taunting them again. The high mocking sound of his voice rang across the valley.

'What's he sayin' now?'

'He says it will soon be dark and the flames of this building will light up the night.'

'We coulda avoided all this.' Black Jack angrily tried to wrench his handcuffs apart. 'We're all gonna burn alive an' they're gonna take the women anyway.'

Doc moved the counter away from the door to allow him to open it a crack. He called out in Paiute.

'Whatcha sayin', Doc?' Dixie said.

'I asked him if he wants some more whiskey. I said I kin get 'im some.'

'Don't you go out there, Doc,' Dixie implored.

'He's drunk now,' Doc said. 'If I kin get 'im to take a few bottles o' my red-eye, maybe we kin get outa here.'

'What's to stop 'im putting an arrow through you soon

as you walk out that door?' Frenchie said.

'Look,' Doc said, 'he wanted to burn us out, he coulda already done it. If I kin get 'im thinking about the whiskey for a while, it might buy us a little time.'

The Paiute voice called again. Doc shouted something in reply.

Doc turned to Dixie. 'He's given me till dusk to get the whiskey. That's about two hours.'

'I don' like it,' Zac said. 'How're you gonna bring the whiskey back?'

'How do we know he's gonna come back?' Black Jack said. 'You'all don' know what he's bin sayin'. He coulda invited the damn Paiute in fer breakfast, while he hightails it down to Sacramento, for all we know.'

'I'm warnin' you,' Dixie snapped. 'You kin still say that after yesterday?'

Black Jack fell silent.

'Wait,' Virgil said. He gestured them all to be quiet. 'Hear that?'

Everyone strained to listen.

'I hear it,' Black Jack said. 'Know what that means?'

'Means we gotta quit all this talkin' an' do somethin' fast.'

'The're stackin' the wood up against the back wall again, ain't they?' Lisa May sobbed. 'They wouldn't do that if they wasn't planning on burnin' us out.'

'You ain't sayin' nothin', Doc,' Dixie said. 'That's what's got me worried. Usually you say them Paiute are jus' playin' with us. You ain't said it this time.'

'I'll go get 'em alla my whiskey. I kin bring it down on the mule I got up at my place. Should be able to make it back by nightfall. Then tonight, when they got a gutfull, we'll slip out into the woods. Maybe we kin make it back down to Sacramento. Ain't nothing else we kin do.

'There's an old stone-built Spanish farm buildin' about a mile east of the Sacramento road,' Doc continued. 'Been empty since 'forty-nine. We could maybe make it as far as that in one night. Rest up during the day an' head out the nex' night.'

'You don' think these Paiute'll be able to track us, even if we do manage to slip past 'em tonight?' Black Jack sneered.

'I'm gonna leave you my shotgun,' Doc said. 'They ain't gonna hurt me when I'm on the way to get the whiskey. I got another one up at my cabin. I'll bring that back down with me.'

'You reckon them braves are gonna let you back in here? They gonna scalp you right there in the street with us all watchin',' Black Jack said

'You talk too much,' Doc said. 'An' I ain't heard no one come up with a better plan.'

'I'll come out with ya,' Zac said suddenly. 'You head off outa town to get the whiskey. They'll be watchin' you. I'll run across the street to the hardware store. If there's guns an' ammo over there, we gotta get it. I'll be able to make it back all right.' Zac looked around for support, but no one spoke. No one caught his eye.

'What weapons we got?' Tom said. 'I got a pistol an' a scattergun, a belt o' ammo an' fourteen shells for the scattergun.'

'I got a Colt, so's Dixie. Doc's got a scattergun with two shells,' Zac said.

'That all?' Tom looked anxiously from one face to the other. 'Ain't you got nothin', Frenchie?'

'Gived my gun to Dixie,' he said. 'Got a throwin' knife an' a derringer.'

'What about you, Virgil?'

'Left my scattergun tied on my mule when I ran in here,' Virgil said quietly.

'Jeez,' Tom breathed. 'Two Colts, a shotgun with two shots in it, a knife an' a derringer between the six o' you.'

'This fool took my guns away,' Black Jack nodded at Zac.

'I gotta get goin',' Doc said. 'Them Paiute braves ain't wanna wait much longer.'

Doc handed his shotgun to Frenchie. He shifted the counter away from the door and pulled the door open. He called out something in Paiute and waited. There was no reply. Doc pushed through the partly opened door, Zac followed right behind him, his Colt in his hand.

Standing to one side of the Express Office window, Tom watched Doc stride up the street towards the edge of town. Keeping low, Zac ran towards the overturned wagon in the middle of the street and ducked down behind it. Doc quickened his pace. Zac waited until Doc was past the last building and out of town. Glancing anxiously round, Zac stood up, ready to carry on across the street to the hardware store. An arrow struck him in the chest.

Zac remained standing and stared straight ahead of him for a moment. Then he fell backwards. His Colt dropped beside him on the road.

Doc carried on walking.

12

Tom reeled. He clutched at the window sill to hold himself up.

'What is it?' Dixie was standing behind him. She caught her breath and pulled Tom down, below the line of the window, against the flour sacks. She looked at the others.

'Zac's caught an arrow.'

'Is he. . . ?' Gracie began.

'Well, he sure ain't movin',' Dixie said.

'Now we got one gun less,' Black Jack said.

'What about Doc?' Virgil asked, holding tight on to Lisa May.

Tom stood up again and peered through the window and up the street. 'Can't see 'im.'

'Maybe they're gonna let him do a trade. Us for the whiskey. Doncha think?' Lisa May looked at Dixie. 'I mean, Doc knows they Injuns, don't he? He's traded with them before.'

Dixie didn't answer her.

'You gotta give me a gun,' Black Jack said.

'I ain't givin' you nothin',' Tom said.

Black Jack looked at him sharply. 'Why not?'

'I'm keepin' my pistol. The scattergun I'm givin' to one of the girls.' He turned to them. 'Which one o' you can shoot best?'

'I can,' Lisa May said.

Tom handed her the shotgun.

'You crazy?' Black Jack said. 'You know I kin shoot better than anyone in here. Don' tell me you're after the goddam reward.'

'Nope,' Tom said. 'I don't give a damn about that. Reason I come back here, is because I come after you. You shot my brother in cold blood.'

'What? Who are you anyways? I seen you around White Fir, but I never done nothin' to you.'

'You an' your boys jumped him, took his gold. When he wanted it back, you shot him.'

'You got your story all twisted, mister,' Black Jack said. He stared into Tom's eyes. 'I never took no gold off no one. Only gold I had, me 'n my boys panned fer up on Honey River. Whole town knows we went up there. Some young fella tried to get my gold off me, so I took a shot at 'im. Anyone woulda done the same.'

'You two better quit yabberin' an' think about what we're gonna do if the Doc don't come back,' Dixie said suddenly. Then something caught her attention. 'What was that?'

Everyone strained to hear. She looked at the others. A low, unearthly moan came from outside.

'Ain't Doc, is it?' she said.

Then they heard clearly. Zac was calling out for Tom. It was a weak, pitiful sound. 'Help me, Tom. You gotta pull me inside. You gotta help me.'

Tom and Dixie stood up and peered round the edge of

the window. Zac was lifting his head and saw them. 'Tom, you gotta get me inside.'

'Don't you even think about it,' Dixie hissed. 'You take one step outside this door an' you're a dead man. We need you in here to protect the girls.'

Gracie whimpered. She pressed herself against Dixie.

'Tom,' Zac's voice implored. 'You gotta help me. Tom, kin you hear me?' His head dropped back on to the ground.

'Jus' lay still,' Tom hissed. 'They won't do nothing so long as they think you're dead. They see you movin', they gonna take another shot at you.'

Zac moaned, a low sound like an injured animal, the breath catching in his throat. Everyone inside the Express office listened in horror. Gracie covered her ears with her shaking hands.

'Tom, you gotta get me inside so's Doc kin take a look at me.' He picked up his head again. An arrow thudded into the ground a foot from Zac's shoulder. 'They're gonna kill me, Tom,' he moaned.

'Lie still,' Tom hissed again. 'I'm tryin to think what to do. Jus' quit movin' aroun'.'

'They're keepin him alive 'cos they want you to go out there,' Dixie said. 'They coulda finished him off easy if they'da wanted to.'

Gracie began to rock back and forth, sobbing with every breath. Her eyes were tight shut and her hands clasped over her ears. Everyone in the room looked at her. Virgil pushed himself into the corner and pulled Lisa May hard against him, shielding her with his arm. Black Jack stared at Gracie for a few moments, then turned his head away. Dixie and Tom continued to watch Zac from round the side of the window.

'Tom.' Zac's voice was weaker this time. 'What's that noise?'

'It ain't nothing. It's just Gracie. She don't feel good is all,' Tom said. 'You just shut up an' lie still now.'

'Tom, it's gettin' cold out here. You gotta git me inside so's I kin warm up.'

Dixie held Tom's arm firmly. 'You ain't goin' nowhere,' she hissed.

Grey clouds gathered over the mountains. A misty rain washed across White Fir as afternoon turned towards evening. Zac lay silent and still. The street became clagging mud all around him. Tom and Dixie could not tell if he was still alive.

They waited. An hour seemed like a day. None of them spoke. Gracie continued to rock back and forth with her eyes tight shut and her hands over her ears. She was whining now, a single, high, unearthly note. Dixie patted her shoulder and tried to hush her. A rat skittered across the floor somewhere at the back of the office. The tiny sound made them all look up. Tom stood beside the window keeping watch for Doc. Outside, the weather was getting worse. The evening rain swept over Zac and the sky darkened.

Dixie joined Tom at the window again.

'What happened yesterday?' Tom asked.

Dixie glanced down at Gracie, who was still holding her head in her hands, rocking back and forth.

'We was loading the wagon,' Dixie began. 'We let Gracie sit up on it. She wasn't no help with the work. She was just cryin' an' shakin' an' all. The rest of us was out the back lookin' for supplies. Injuns rode in faster 'n lightning.

No one had time to do nothin'. Nex' thing we know, they start ridin' round the wagon, shoutin' an' pointin' at Gracie. She was screamin'. Willy came runnin' out with his shotgun.'

Dixie paused and stared straight ahead of her out of the window, as if she was seeing what had happened over again.

'Injuns heaved the wagon over. Gracie an' Willy was caught underneath. Wagon landed on Willy's shoulder. His arm was stickin' out. He was howlin' fit to call the devil. Gracie was screamin'. Both of 'em underneath. We all ran out. Zac was shootin'. Frenchie was shootin'. Injuns'd rode up to the end of the street by that time. Zac reckons he got one of 'em.'

'Jeez,' Tom said.

'Then one of 'em pulled 'is horse roun' an' rode right back at us. Zac an' Frenchie was tryin' to reload. We had to dive outa the way. Right there in front of us, he reached down, grabbed Willy's arm that was stickin' out from under the wagon 'an pulled it right off. He was laughin' an' whoopin' like it was a game. He jest threw it in the air back over his shoulder.'

'No one managed to shoot 'im?' Tom said.

'Frenchie said he winged 'im. But I dunno. He never came off his horse. Tell you what though, I ain't never seen no one ride so fast.'

'Jeez. What did ya do then? Tipped up the wagon?'

'Yeah, we all did. There was Gracie goin' outa her mind. Her fingers was all bloody where she'd bin tryin' to tear her way out. There was Willy. Gracie'd bin lyin' right next to him.'

'What happened to Willy?'

'We brung 'im inside. Laid 'im down. After that he bled to death real quick.'

'Where is he now?'

'We put 'im out the back with the supplies, so we didn't have to look at 'im.'

'I'm sick o' this,' Virgil said suddenly. He pushed Lisa May aside and stood up. 'I can't take no more jus' sittin''. I gotta do somethin'.'

'Yeah?' Dixie said. 'Like what, exactly?'

'I'm a photographer,' Virgil said. 'I'm gonna take your photograph.'

'What?'

'Take your picture. I ain't got nothin' else to do. I got all my gear right here.' He started untying a bundle wrapped in oilcloth.'

'You crazy?'

'Nope. You got any better ideas? If we get outta this, your picture's gonna be on the front page of the *California Daily Star.* If we don't, well, then at least they'll be able to tell who was here.'

'The hell with the *California Daily Star.* I jus' wanna stay alive.'

Virgil froze. They all heard it. Zac was calling out again. His voice seemed stronger.

'Whatcha doin', Tom? Why ain'tcha come for me? Somethin' happened to ya?'

Gracie started to moan again, her eyes shut, her hands over her ears.

Dixie held her gun against Tom's leg. 'You even think of goin' out there, I'm gonna shoot you in the leg. That way you'll still be able to shoot Injuns when they come fer us. You go out there, you're a dead man.'

Tom called to Zac. 'You jus' lie still now, Zac. I'll come fer you when it's dark. You jus' be patient now. Don't you move now.'

'It's dark as hell now, Tom. Ain'tcha gonna come fer me?' Zac's voice seemed to turn into the whine of a beaten dog as waves of pain swept through him.

Lisa May began to cry. Deep, heart-felt sobs of grief poured out from within her.

Virgil put down his box of lenses and sat down to comfort her. Gracie opened her eyes for a second and stared at Lisa May. Then she covered her ears against the sound of her friend crying, still rocking back and forth. Dixie's arm rested across her shoulders.

'Jeez,' Black Jack said. 'I can't take no more o' this. You're damn cowards alla ya.' He turned to Tom. 'You got the damn gall to accuse me o' killin', when that's exactly what you're doin'. That damn fool out there's gonna die if you don't help him. That makes you no better'n me.'

'You shut up,' Dixie said. 'That damn fool out there's gonna die anyway an' you know it. He took his chances trying to do right. That's somethin' you wouldn't understand. Anyhow, if you're so goddam brave, you go out there and drag him in. You wanna do that an' I'll open the door fer you myself.'

Black Jack laughed. 'Me? I ain't fetchin' him. That's the fella wants to take me down to Sacramento and claim the reward. He kin rot in hell fer all I care.'

Tom leapt across the room, drew back his fist and slugged Black Jack in the face. 'You jus' can it,' Tom yelled. 'I swear if you say one more word, I'm gonna tear your head off.'

Black Jack spat out a mouthful of blood and a broken

tooth. 'You coward. If that was my frien' lyin' out there in the rain dyin', I wouldn't be sat in here because some saloon belle said she'd shoot me in the leg.'

Tom drew his Colt, cocked it and pointed it at Cheetham's head. 'One more thing. Go on. Say jus' one more thing.'

Gracie snapped. She jumped to her feet, screaming. Dixie tried to grab her flailing arms. Gracie's eyes were tight shut. No one understood what she was trying to do. Before anyone could get to her, she had heaved the oak counter back eighteen inches, squeezed round it and opened the door. She felt the air on her face and stopped screaming. Tom made a grab for her as she stepped outside.

'No one ain't helpin' him,' Gracie shouted at them. She bunched her fists like a child about to explode into a tantrum.

'Look what you done now,' Black Jack spat.

Lisa May and Dixie yelled for her to stop. She turned at the familiar sound of their voices and looked at them for a moment, but appeared not to see them. Jack made another lunge for her but tripped against the counter. Gracie had a polite and distant smile on her face as if she was being introduced to people she did not know. She pulled the door closed after her.

Inside, everyone was shouting. Jack and Virgil fell over each other trying to get round the counter to the door. Lisa May was sobbing. Dixie was banging on the window and shouting to Gracie to come back.

The cool rain swept across Gracie's face. She stepped calmly forward, seeming not to notice she was wearing only one shoe, down the steps on to the muddy street.

Tom wrenched the door open and dived after her. A hail of arrows landed in the ground in front of him, making him stop short. He yelled to Gracie, imploring her to come back.

Gracie was in the middle of the street now, stepping calmly forward with deliberate trance-like steps. Tom took a step towards her and an arrow caught him in the shoulder. The force of it kicked him backwards. Pain burned into him like a branding-iron. Dixie was screaming at him from the doorway. Virgil threw himself down the steps and dragged Tom back inside.

Gracie looked down at Zac, lying in the mud. He said something to her which she appeared to hear. Dixie was still banging on the window. Gracie hesitated for a moment as if she were listening to a sound which came from far away. Then she bent down, slipped her hands under Zac's shoulders and tried to drag him back towards the Express office door. She tried, but she couldn't lift his shoulders off the ground.

Everyone inside was shouting. Gracie recognized nothing. The voices of people she knew, cries for her to come back, even the sound of her own name made no impression. Gracie stood up and turned back towards the office window. An empty smile was written across her pale face. An arrow struck her in the back. The force of it knocked her forward, face down into the mud.

Dixie wailed in despair. Rain washed across the street.

Tom was slumped against the wall with the arrow sticking out of his shoulder. He was pale and his face glowed with a sheen of perspiration. He forced himself to his feet.

'Don't be a fool,' Dixie said.

Tom thrust his gun into her hand.

Tom opened the door and, ducking low, ran over to Zac and Gracie. He felt for a pulse on Gracie's slim neck. Then he grabbed Zac under his arms and hauled him back through the mud. Virgil ran down the steps to help him get Zac inside. They laid Zac on the floor. Frenchie found an old sack for them to use as a pillow. Dixie knelt over him. But he was already dead.

Tom collapsed. The effort of dragging Zac in combined with loss of blood was too much.

'He make it?' Tom gasped. 'He was alive out there.'

Dixie shook her head. 'He ain't now.'

Tom lay sprawled against the counter, the arrow still lodged in his shoulder. 'Frenchie, lay 'im down flat,' Dixie said. 'An' you,' she pointed to Black Jack, 'gimme that belt.'

Black Jack struggled to unbuckle his leather belt with his cuffed hands. Dixie folded the belt into three and pushed it roughly into Tom's mouth.

'You,' she nodded to Lisa May. 'Make sure he don't spit it out. You,' she said to Black Jack. 'When I say, you put your foot on 'is chest an' hold 'im down hard.'

Dixie tore cotton strips from her petticoats.

They lay Tom on the floor beside Zac's body. Virgil held his shoulders; Frenchie held his legs; Lisa May kept the leather belt in his mouth; Black Jack pressed down with his foot on Tom's chest. Dixie grabbed the arrow with both hands and yanked it out of his shoulder. Even with the belt to bite down on, Tom bellowed like a stuck pig and reared up against them all. As the tension flooded out of Tom's body, they let go of him and he passed into unconsciousness.

As Dixie bound up Tom's shoulder, lightning flickered

across the mountains. Rain drummed hard on the Express office roof. Virgil went back to setting up his camera, the dish of magnesium powder and the fuse. The others sat on the floor, staring blankly in front of them. It was dusk now. Grey evening light drained the colour out of everything.

'Dixie,' Lisa May said softly. 'Can't you see nothin' of Doc?'

'He'll be comin' soon,' she said.

13

Two hours earlier, Lynchburg stood at the side of the track contemplating the mess. Smashed demijohns and broken bottles were everywhere. Pieces of a wooden crate were strewn around. A length of good rope had been thrown down and a mule grazed, untethered, on the verge. The place smelled of sour whiskey. He had seen a man head up this track on foot an hour before. Now there was no one about.

Lynchburg had come up to White Fir to collect Cheetham and claim the reward. He knew it was risky. But a young guy he had met in Sacramento had disappeared suddenly. Lynchburg knew that he had heard about the reward. Then there was talk of an army unit moving on the place. Lynchburg had to make sure he got to Cheetham before someone else did.

He had left his horse hidden a little way off the roadside where the undergrowth was thick and made his way up to White Fir on foot. Hiding in the brush, at the edge of town, he saw two men come out of the Pony Express office. Lynchburg recognized the miners' leader but did not know the older man who headed out of town on foot.

The miners' leader was clearly trying to make it to the building across the street. Lynchburg saw him taken down by a Paiute arrow when he reached the middle of the road. Lynchburg's stomach lurched. He stayed hidden.

Lynchburg had left Black Jack Cheetham in the charge of the guy who now lay dying in the middle of the street. if Black Jack was still alive, he figured, he must be inside the Pony Express office. But he wasn't about to put himself within range of the Paiute arrows to find out. He decided to wait for dark, then he could short-cut through the bushes and join the track the old guy had followed, up towards the claims. He could find out what had happened to Cheetham from him. If Black Jack was dead, Lynchburg would head straight back to Sacramento. He sat back to wait.

Night fell quickly. It was raining. Lynchburg was just about to make a move when someone lit an oil lamp in the Express office. Fools, he thought, to make themselves a target like that. For the moment, there was no sign of the Paiute on the other side of the valley. To be safe, he decided to stay where he was a while longer. He expected the attack would come at first light.

Frenchie broke the chain which linked Cheetham's wrists with a hammer and chisel he found in the storeroom.

'About time,' Black Jack said. 'I coulda done somethin' if that fool bounty hunter hadn't trussed me like a damn chicken.'

'Shaddup,' Dixie said. 'Ain't no one feels sorry fer you. Let's jus' get on with it, while we're still breathin'.'

Black Jack and Frenchie set to work levering a plank out of the back wall.

'Light one o' those oil lamps,' Black Jack said. 'I can't see a damn thing.'

'We hang some sacks up in fronta the window an' light a lamp just before we sneak outa here. Not before,' Dixie said. 'It'll draw their attention.'

The men worked as quietly as they could, but the pine boards had been nailed in hard. Eventually, one gave way with a loud crack. They all froze, trying to figure out whether the sound had carried. Nothing happened, so the men began to work at a second board. With two boards out, there was a gap in the planks at the back of the building big enough for them to squeeze through one at a time.

'I'll take his gun,' Black Jack said. He nodded towards Tom.

'No,' Tom opened his eyes. 'I still got my right hand. I kin still shoot.'

'He's too weak,' Black Jack said, looking round to the others.

'It's his gun,' Dixie said. 'Frenchie, you take yours back an' I'll take Lisa May's shotgun.'

'Come on,' Virgil said. He picked up Tom's scattergun. 'I'll go first.'

Virgil pushed his way out through the space between the planks and shoved aside the pile of soaking wet brushwood, to make a way for the others. He stood still and listened. The only sound was trees stirring in the wind and rain sweeping over the leaves. He whispered for the others to follow. Lisa was next, then Black Jack, Frenchie and Tom. Dixie lit an oil lamp before she ducked out between the planks.

Virgil led them in single file behind the buildings and piles of collapsed tents. Within minutes their clothes were soaked through. Tom stumbled but managed to stay on his feet. The darkness disorientated them. They could feel the ground sloping away and, if they looked back, they could make out the yellow glow of Dixie's oil lamp which showed them where they had come from. Apart from that, they couldn't tell where they were.

At the edge of town, Virgil led them out on to the muddy road. They could move faster here than if they tried to push their way through the undergrowth. Frenchie supported Tom, under his arm. The others walked blind with their arms stretched out in front of them. There was no moon and the darkness was so thick that they couldn't see each other. The main problem was staying on the road. Virgil kept leading them off into the undergrowth where they tripped and fell. Their hands and elbows were cut and bruised. Branches whipped their faces.

The darkness dissolved time and distance. No one knew how long they had been walking. Once they were out of sight of the oil lamp, they couldn't tell how far they had gone. They only knew that they were going downhill and that somewhere ahead of them was the old stone farmstead which they had to find by daybreak. Fear drove them on.

Eventually, they felt the gradient begin to flatten out. The rain had eased now. Virgil called out for them to stop. They sat down where they were. Frenchie let Tom lean against him.

'How is he?' Dixie said.

'He ain't sayin' much,' Frenchie said. 'But his legs are still movin'.'

'I'm doin' fine,' Tom said. Dixie heard how weak his voice was.

'Guess he must be losin' a lotta blood,' Frenchie said.

'No way we kin tell where to turn off the road to head for the farmhouse 'fore it gets light,' Virgil said.

'Doc said there was a track,' Dixie said.

'It'll be overgrown,' Virgil said. 'Ain't no one used the place fer years, that's what he said.'

'What d'you reckon happened to Doc?' Lisa May's voice was dull with fear and fatigue.

'Don't you worry about him,' Dixie said sharply. 'Doc's lived up here for years.'

'We gonna go on, or what?' Black Jack said.

Frenchie pulled Tom to his feet. Tom's head swam. He leaned heavily on Frenchie. 'I'm OK,' he said.

'Be light in an hour,' Frenchie said. 'We'll get to the farmhouse. Then we kin rest up.'

They looked behind them. The first grey streaks of day had appeared over the Sierras.

'They ain't gonna follow us now, are they?' Lisa May said. 'Not out here.'

'Let's get movin',' Dixie said.

Lynchburg pulled his hat down low and turned up the collar of his waterproof. He sat under a tree with his Colt in his hand. Sleep tempted him now. He fought to stay awake. He had spent two hours staring out into the darkness unable to see anything but the yellow light from the Express office window and unable to hear anything but the spring rain washing over the trees.

Suddenly, an unearthly, silent explosion lit up the valley. It came from inside the Express office. The silhouettes of a dozen Paiute braves gathered round the door were imprinted on the darkness. Lynchburg recoiled with shock. The magnesium flash terrified the braves and they yelled and scrambled over each other to get away. Lynchburg heard them running back across the muddy street, shouting in terror.

Lynchburg stood up, shaking the stiffness and the cold out of his limbs. Now was the time to get over to the Express office. He might be able to get everyone out, before the Paiute came back. He figured they must have run out of ammo to be forced to frighten the Indians away with a magnesium flare. He ran over to the building, treading lightly and keeping low. As he climbed the steps, he called out to whoever was inside. He was surprised to receive no answer. He called again. They must have heard him.

He pushed open the door, calling softly. He was amazed to find the room empty. The lamp stood on a table by the window and a camera stood on its tripod facing the door. A length of string attached to the door had pulled a burning fuse across the magnesium dish next to the camera. A second string had opened the shutter. Lynchburg smiled.

'I'll be damned.'

Virgil stopped and pointed.

'There it is.'

The others peered into the gloom and could just make out the tumbled-down walls of an old building, half a mile off the road.

'We're mighty exposed crossin' out there,' Frenchie said. There was open grassland between the road and the house.

'Well, let's get on,' Dixie said. 'It'll be light 'fore we get there.'

They headed out, away from the shadow of the woods. Wet rye grass brushed their legs. Deeper into the field, the grass was above waist height. Streaks of grey light broke open the darkness over the mountains. Tom stumbled now, sometimes missing steps altogether, relying on Frenchie to haul him along. Dixie kept glancing back. No one was following.

As they approached the broken walls of the farmstead, a figure stepped out of the shadows. Frenchie raised his gun fast.

'Don' shoot, don' shoot,' the figure hissed. 'I seen you comin' from the road.'

It was Doc. He gestured them behind the walls of the building. They threw themselves down, exhausted.

'How come you're here?' Dixie threw her arms around him. 'I thought them Paiute were gonna finish you, Doc.'

Doc chuckled. 'It's like I tol' you. They're jus' young bucks all fired up. You got anythin' to eat?'

'We got some pemmican outa the Pony Express office.'

'I dunno. The grease in that stuff turns in my stomach,' Doc said. 'I'll pass. We got a well fulla fresh water here though.'

'Ain't bad?' Black Jack said. 'I heard Injuns poisoned the wells o' farmsteads like this.'

'Folks'll say anythin',' Doc said. 'The Paiute'd never do nothing like that.'

'Well, I'm gonna haul some up. I got a ragin' thirst on me. I'll bring a bucket in then we kin all have a drink.'

'You best take a look at him,' Dixie said indicating Tom.

Frenchie had propped him against the wall. His eyes were closed. His breathing was fast and shallow. In the gathering light, they could see that the front of his shirt was soaked in blood.

'Took an arrow in the shoulder,' Dixie said.

Doc gently unbuttoned the shirt, pulled it open and unwrapped the petticoat bandage. Doc caught his breath as he looked down on the wound.

'I pulled it out,' Dixie said. 'I didn't know what else to do. I jus' tried to make it quick.'

Doc grunted.

'Gotta clean it. Then I kin dress it proper. Someone's gotta light a fire. I gotta have hot water.'

Virgil started to gather odd bits of wood and pile them up. Black Jack set a bucket of water down for them all.

'Whatcha doin'? You can't build no fire here. You'll tell every damn Injun fer miles aroun' where we are.'

'They already know,' Doc said. 'Don'cha think they saw ya leave White Fir?'

'Hell no,' Black Jack said. 'We made a hole in the back wall an' sneaked out. If they'da seen us, we wouldn't be here now.'

'You jus' don' get it, do you? You're jus' like all the others.' Doc sighed. 'This is Paiute territory. They see everything that happens.' He paused. 'Them braves let you walk outa there because they had a reason to. I don' know what in the hell it was, but they had one all right.'

Everyone silently listened to Doc.

'Them braves is outa control for a while. The older fellas from the tribe are tryin' to rein 'em in. When I went up to get the hooch, some o' the old guys was waitin' fer me on the road an' smashed all the jars. Tol' me I wasn't to trade no more liquor. I gived 'em my word.'

'You're always makin' excuses for 'em,' Black Jack said. 'Them's all savages to me.'

'You know what started all this, doncha? Some damn guys comin' in from the East on a wagon train took after a bunch o' Paiute women over by Lake Tahoe. That's what made the braves kick off.'

'Well?' Black Jack said. 'Lake Tahoe ain't here. None of us ain't harmed no Paiute women.'

Doc held in his anger. 'We're all white men. That way, they figure it's all our fault.' Doc paused. 'The older guys, on the other hand, know that if they can't control the young bucks, the army'll come in an' they'll have a full-scale Indian war on their hands.'

'Damn right,' Black Jack said. 'I wish the army was here now.'

'You jus' gotta remember what them guys from the wagon train did. One of 'em was a man of the cloth too, so I heard. Now, build the damn fire or this boy's arm'll git infected.'

Pale daylight pushed across the sky. Clouds threatened rain again. The soft calls of quail sounded across the chaparral. Virgil piled twigs and grass together and made a spark. Flames took hold quickly. Sitting back against a stone wall, Black Jack watched the blue smoke curl up into the air.

'Ain't none of us keeping watch,' Black Jack said. 'If we're gonna announce to 'em we're here, we should at least watch out to see 'em comin'.' He got to his feet. 'I'll take first turn.'

Lisa May was asleep on Dixie's shoulder. Frenchie was slumped beside Tom, keeping him upright against the wall. Virgil knelt on the ground to blow on the fire.

'Where's Gracie?' Doc said, suddenly noticing that someone was missing.

Dixie explained.

Kneeling beside Tom, Doc peered at the wound. 'Part o' the arrow's still in here, Dixie. You gotta dig 'em out. If you pull 'em, they break off. Damn.' He looked round. 'You still got that knife o' yours, Frenchie?'

Frenchie held the knife out to Doc.

'Best sharpen it up,' Doc said.

Frenchie felt in his pocket for his whetstone and spat on it. Everyone watched him slide the blade back and forth.

Doc took a tin cup and a bottle of whiskey from his bag. He handed the cup to Virgil.

'Boil up some water in that,' he said. 'Dixie, I need some fresh bandages.'

While Doc was waiting for the water to boil, he took a deep slug out of the bottle. Dixie caught his eye.

'Steadies my hand,' he said.

14

After digging out the remains of the arrow from Tom's shoulder, Doc splashed the wound with whiskey and bandaged it up. Tom looked sick. His face was pale as wax. Doc mixed up a potion of herbs from his bag and Dixie brought the cup to his lips and encouraged him to drink. Everyone else was asleep except Virgil, who had taken over as look out from Black Jack. It was mid-morning. The sun was high in the sky and the heat of the day had gathered.

They woke with a start. Virgil scrambled down from the lookout post up on the wall.

'Rider comin',' he whispered urgently.

Lisa May's eyes opened in terror. She clutched Dixie's arm tight. 'Injuns?'

'Nope. Jus' one guy.'

Virgil shinned back up the wall to see.

The rider made straight for them.

He rode into the ruined building and dismounted. He unhitched a coil of rope from his saddle and held it in his hand.

He nodded a greeting to each of them. 'Lynchburg,' he said. 'Outa Texas.'

'What're you doin' out here?' Virgil said.

'I come fer him,' Lynchburg said. He drew his gun, a Paterson Colt revolver, and pointed it at Black Jack.

Black Jack gasped and pressed himself back against the wall.

'You the bounty hunter, mister?' Dixie said.

'That's right,' Lynchburg said. 'Good a way to make a livin' as any. What happened to him?' Lynchburg gestured to Tom.

'He took an arrow. Doc patched 'im up.'

Lynchburg sat down against the wall facing Black Jack, still holding his gun. He put the rope down beside him.

'Got any coffee?'

'Ain't got no coffee. We kin offer you a drink o' water,' Dixie said. 'An' we got some pemmican.'

'I can't stand that stuff,' Lynchburg said. 'Makes me retch. I'll take a drink o' water though.'

Lynchburg told them how he had been watching the Pony Express office. He told them about the magnesium flare.

'Brighter than summer lightnin',' he said. 'Throwed a scare into them Paiute. Yes, sir.'

'Hey, it worked.' Virgil said. 'I tell ya, I gotta get that picture. No one's ever taken a picture of the Paiute before. 'Fact, there ain't many've taken a picture with a magnesium flare without burnin' the place down neither. My editor's gonna love me. Those Indians still up there?'

'Can't tell,' Lynchburg said. 'If they were there when I left, they was mighty quiet.'

'One thing's fer sure,' Doc said. 'They were comin' for us in the night. They didn't have no whiskey neither. The elders couldn't have got to 'em.'

'Or they tried,' Dixie said, 'an' the braves wouldn't listen.'

'You can't stay here,' Lynchburg said. 'I could see your trail across the grassland a mile off an' I ain't no Injun tracker.' He paused. 'Fact is, I'm planning on leavin' right now, an' I'm takin' him with me.'

Black Jack glowered. 'Ain't nothin' I'd like better than to get outa here, even if it means puttin' up with scum like you.'

Lynchburg reached inside his jacket with his other hand and tossed the Wanted poster on the ground between them.

'I git you an' I git the full set.'

'What'd'ya mean?' Black Jack said.

Lynchburg cocked his pistol.

'Put these on or I'll shoot you right this second. I see you busted the last pair I gived ya.' He threw a pair of handcuffs over to Black Jack.

'Now, I said,' Lynchburg snarled.

Black Jack put the cuffs on. Everyone heard the click as they locked shut.

'One day soon me an' my boys is gonna turn you into crow bait.' Black Jack spat on the ground at Lynchburg's feet.

Lynchburg laughed. 'Git on yer knees an' face the wall.'

Black Jack did as he was told. Lynchburg holstered his gun and made a noose out of one end of the rope.

'Whoa now, mister,' Dixie said. 'We don't want no necktie party.'

Lynchburg knocked Black Jack's hat off and slipped the noose over his head.

'Now geddup.' Lynchburg held on to the other end of

the rope. He drew his pistol and covered Black Jack again.

'I ain't got two horses,' Lynchburg said. 'So you're jus' gonna have to walk.' He pulled himself up into the saddle.

He turned to Black Jack and tugged on the rope.

Black Jack's head jerked sideways. 'My boys'll git you, you piece o' trash.'

'Too late fer that, my frien'. I caught up with them two lowlifes in a Chinese café in Sacramento. To git my reward I gotta bring you in.' He chuckled. '*Re*-ward says dead or alive, so if you don' walk fast enough, I'm jus' gonna shoot you an' sling you over my saddle. Bring you in thataway.'

He clicked his tongue and urged his horse to walk on. Black Jack stumbled after him. 'Walk to the side of me, where I kin see you. Keep the rope taut now.'

'You killed my boys?' Black Jack said.

'Self *de*-fence, frien'. There's a lotta that in my line o' work. That's why I'm gonna be coverin' you with my pistol every step o' the way.' Lynchburg pulled his hat low over his eyes, against the sun.

Virgil scanned the field around the farmstead. They were surrounded by a sea of chest-high rye grass. To the east, the grass ran up to the road. He could clearly see the track they had made crossing the field during the night. Beyond that there was woodland which became more dense as the slope climbed towards White Fir. There was no sign of human life. The midday sun beat down.

'Can't move 'im.' Doc pointed to Tom. 'Not for a few hours. Anyone wanna go with them?' He nodded towards Lynchburg.

'I'm stayin' with Dixie,' Lisa May said. 'I ain't goin' with no one else.'

'I ain't goin',' Virgil said. 'I gotta get that picture.'

Frenchie looked at Dixie. 'You holdin' up?'

Dixie put her arm round Lisa May's shoulder. 'We're fine.'

'If we wait,' Doc said, 'it would give the Paiute more time to rein the young bucks in. That's what I'm countin' on.' He turned to Tom. His breathing had deepened. Colour was returning to his cheeks. The glassy sweat which had lain over his face had disappeared.

'Lookin' better, ain't he?' Dixie said.

'He'll be fine. That Paiute drink heals damn near everything.'

'What are our chances, Doc?' Dixie said softly.

'If the Paiute elders have reined in the young 'uns, they're pretty good.'

'And if they ain't?'

Doc smiled. 'Well, we're nearer Sacramento than we was last night.'

Frenchie joined Virgil on the wall to watch Lynchburg and Black Jack cross the grassland. Sometimes the grass was so high Black Jack disappeared altogether and only Lynchburg's head and shoulders showed where they were. They had reached the edge of the long grass now and were almost on the road.

Two Paiute braves leapt up out of the grass and yanked Lynchburg off his horse. All Frenchie and Virgil could see was the grass thrashing violently as the men fought on the ground. A shot rang out. The echo rolled around the plain. Then someone was on his feet, head down, running towards them, crashing through the grass. Black Jack had cut loose.

More braves appeared out of the trees on the other side of the road. A hail of arrows were loosed after him but fell short. The braves began to follow but turned back before they were in range of the guns in the farmstead. A minute later, Black Jack threw himself over the wall, his lungs bursting.

'They're everywhere,' he said. 'In the woods. By the road. You can't see 'em from here.'

'What about the other fella?' Doc asked.

Black Jack shook his head. 'Sonofabitch took an arrow in 'is chest. Before they pulled 'im off 'is horse.'

Lisa May clung tight to Dixie.

'We gotta have a guard on both ends o' the building,' Frenchie said. 'Keep all directions covered.'

'They won't come in daylight.' Doc shook his head. He looked down at Tom who was sleeping peacefully.

Virgil and Frenchie kept watch at either end of the building. Black Jack hammered the chain between his handcuffs against a stone block until his wrists bled. Eventually it broke. He unhitched the rope from round his neck, picked up his hat and scrambled up the wall beside Virgil.

An hour passed. The day was at its hottest. Dixie filled the tin cup from the bucket and took it round to the men on lookout. There was no movement out in the grassland. The rasp of cicadas filled the glassy air.

They could see the trail where Black Jack had run back and the patch where Lynchburg had come off his horse. A warm breeze lifted the leaves of the oaks and maples on the other side of the road and made the tall grass sway like the sea.

'Anybody want some of this pemmican?' Dixie said. 'It'll go rotten in this heat, if it ain't already.'

'Pass it round,' Doc said. 'We gotta eat somethin'.'

Dixie unwrapped the hunk of grease and meat and cut it up with Frenchie's knife.

'Smells bad an' tastes worse,' she said. 'Means gotta be doin' you some good. That's what my ma used to say.'

Doc mixed up another potion. He supported Tom's head while Lisa held the mug to his lips.

Tom spluttered. 'What's that you're givin' me? Tastes like dirt.'

'He's on the mend,' Doc said.

'You should try this damn pemmican,' Dixie said. 'Tastes like hell on a hot day.'

'How long I bin out?' Tom said.

'Long enough to start healin',' Doc said. 'I took what's lefta the arrow outa your shoulder. You jus' lay back an' rest while you can.'

'Nobody see nothin'?' Frenchie called from the back wall.

'Only thing movin' out here is a buncha rabbits an' the grass in the wind,' Virgil called back.

'What d'ya think, Doc?' Dixie asked.

'Hard to say,' Doc said. 'We best not stay here too long after nightfall, jus' to be certain. If them braves are there, they'll be thinkin' we'll head back the way we come, straight to the road. Maybe we ought to head out in the other direction. All depends on whether the elders got to 'em yet. If they have, we ain't got nothin' to worry about.'

'What about Tom? He gonna be able to walk?'

'Some, I guess.'

Black Jack offered to relieve Frenchie on the back wall. Frenchie climbed down, helped himself to a drink of water and slumped down beside the others. He slipped a pack of cards out of his pocket and began to riffle it. He looked at Dixie.

'I'll be able to get us another stake as soon as I git down to Sacramento.'

'We're gonna need it,' Dixie said. 'I want somethin' good this time. A real wood-built dance hall, with a piano in it an' a polished-oak bar. We gotta have a kitchen out back so's we kin serve food all day.'

'I ain't workin' in no kitchen,' Lisa May said.

' 'Course you ain't, darlin', you're my piano player.' She squeezed Liza's shoulder.

'So's when I git in the mood, I kin sing all night. We'll hire a Chinese cook for the kitchen. We'll pay him real good an' he'll cook the best food in the whole o' the Sierras. We'll have stewed liver an' mutton cutlets one day an' then salt pork an' cabbage the next. An' he'll make blueberry pies with all kindsa fruit.'

The men were silent. They smiled to themselves, enjoying Dixie's reverie.

'An' we'd have dancers. Girls would come up from Sacramento an' San Francisco an' would put on dancin' shows. Real tasteful an' nice.'

'Sure would like to see that,' Doc chuckled.

'I might even dance again myself,' Dixie said.

'You were a dancer?' Lisa May said.

'Sure I was,' Dixie said. 'Used to dance the tarantella in burlesque shows back East, when I was about your age.'

'I never seen no one dance the tarantella,' Doc said.

'It's a spider dance,' Dixie explained.

'Oh,' Doc said and tried to imagine it.

'You forgot the tables,' Frenchie added. 'There'd be gamin' tables. So anyone who wanted could play a little faro or a hand o' poker.'

'I ain't forgot 'em,' Dixie said. 'I just ain't mentioned 'em. You couldn't have no dance hall without gamin' tables.'

'Where you gonna find the girls from?' Virgil asked.

Lisa May caught his eye.

'I know places,' Dixie said. 'There's plenty o' girls in California want to make somethin' of themselves.'

'I aim to make somethin' o' myself,' Lisa May said. 'If it wasn't fer Dixie, I'd be scrubbin' floors back East.'

'That's why we're all here, ain't it?'

Everyone looked at Jack. He had propped himself up on one elbow.

'That's why all the miners left their families at home,' he continued. 'That's why they spend every day up to their waist in river water or way down some shaft in the ground.'

'Difference is,' Dixie said, 'that if you're a man you kin make somethin' of yourself whether you come out West or not. You just got a chance of getting real rich out here. If you're a woman an' you stay back East, like Lisa May says, you jus' gonna end up scrubbin'.'

'Best we all get some shut-eye,' Doc said. 'We got the afternoon to rest up. We ain't got nothing to worry about while the sun's shinin'.'

15

Virgil's shots woke them. Then they heard the war whoops of the Paiute braves. Lisa May screamed. Dixie grabbed Tom's Colt out of his holster and scrambled up the wall. Doc picked up his scattergun.

'Ain't no one comin' from the back,' Frenchie yelled.

The braves had formed a wide semicircle and were charging on foot from the direction of the road. They were keeping low and the high grass made them impossible to see.

'You gotta give me a gun,' Black Jack yelled.

Lisa May picked up Tom's scattergun and crawled up the broken wall to join Dixie.

'I can't see 'em,' Virgil yelled. An arrow sliced the air past his head. He fired off round after round into the greenery.

Every time the grass moved, they were tempted to shoot. Their eyes were everywhere but they saw nothing.

Then there was a ferocious yell. A fusiillade of bullets screamed through the air. Lynchburg stood up above the level of the grass, near where he had disappeared. An arrow was lodged in his chest. His bloody face was twisted with fear and fury. He waved his Colt revolver rifie in his right hand and fired off rounds without taking aim. As they watched from the building, a second arrow lodged in his side then a third. He stopped firing and tried to call out but seemed to choke on his words. He spat out a shower of blood and fell back into the greenery.

A Paiute brave scrambled up the wall next to Lisa May and made a grab for her. He gripped a knife between his teeth. Lisa May screamed. Dixie was pushing shells into the chamber of the Colt. Lisa swung the scattergun round and loosed off both barrels. The brave's eyes opened wide with surprise as he pitched over backwards. His knife clattered down the stone wall.

Another young brave was following. He reached the top of the wall and kicked Lisa and Dixie aside. They fell back, clutching at the jagged stones and each other to try to keep their balance. As she stumbled, Dixie's trigger finger tightened and she fired the pistol into the air. The brave leapt over them and landed in front of Tom. Tom scrabbled for his gun but the holster was empty. The brave snatched the knife from his teeth and lunged at him. Then, with the roar of a wild bear, Black Jack hurled himself off the front wall. He landed on top of the brave, grabbed his head between his hands and banged the back of his skull on the stony ground. The brave pushed his way out from under Black Jack and staggered to his feet. While he still reeled with pain and confusion, Black Jack picked him up and, with a huge effort, heaved him bodily back over the wall.

Frenchie yelled. They turned to the back of the farmstead. A line of Paiute, twenty strong, was riding towards them, spears lowered for a charge. Their pace quickened to a gallop. Some of them were raising their bows, as they rode, ready to aim. Frenchie ducked down behind the wall and fired wildly. The earth shook as hoofbeats drummed over the ground, covering the sound of shouts and gunfire. The ponies smashed through the scrub and grass. The riders hollered out war cries.

Behind the walls, Lisa was searching Tom's pockets for more shells. Dixie was firing. Black Jack had run back to be beside Frenchie and was standing on the wall hurling rocks at the riders. Tom was sitting up still searching round for his gun. Virgil was covering the front. He shouted something, but no one seemed to understand. Then Doc's voice cut through.

'They're ridin' past. They ain't comin' fer us.'

Dixie and Lisa, on the side wall, lowered their weapons as the Paiute band thundered past. The braves who had been hidden in the long grass leapt up, shouting with fear, and ran for the woods. Two of them made it. The rest were caught by the riders and herded like cattle across the field and on to the road. Then they were driven up the slope in the direction of White Fir. The terrified braves ran ahead of the riders.

From the edge of the field, one of the riders turned and raised an arm in salute. Doc waved back.

'He's tellin us it's taken care of,' Doc said.

'You mean we kin go back to White Fir?' Virgil asked.

'We ain't goin' back, are we?' Lisa May turned to Dixie.

Dixie smiled at her. 'Not right now. We'll wait till things have quietened down.'

'I gotta get that picture,' Virgil said.

'Jus' be patient, son,' Doc said. 'If you put a scare into 'em like the fella said, ain't none of 'em goin' back into that Express office for a good while.'

Doc dipped the tin cup into the bucket of water and passed it round. They sat, slumped against the walls, exhausted.

'I'm keepin' watch,' Black Jack announced. 'I don' trust these Injuns.' He climbed up the front wall again.

'We should rest up,' Doc said. 'While the day's hot.'

Dixie pushed more shells into the chamber of the Colt. 'No sense in holdin' on to a gun that ain't loaded.'

Black Jack shouted from the wall. 'Riders comin'. A whole bunch of 'em.'

Virgil scrabbled up the wall to join him. 'He's right. You kin see the dust trail. They're comin' up the Sacramento road.'

Doc joined them on the wall. He looked puzzled. 'Ain't the Paiute, comin from that direction.'

After a few minutes, Doc chuckled. 'See that?' He pointed to the group of riders. 'You could just make out flashes through the cloud of dust, as the sunlight glinted off metal. It's the damn cavalry. They got wagons with 'em too.'

The column halted in precise formation on the road opposite the farmhouse. The early afternoon sun flashed on their sabres. Two officers rode across the field on perfectly groomed black stallions. When they got close, they reined in their horses and saluted.

'Captain John Stearne, Commanding Officer First Division, Fourth Brigade, Sutter's Rifles.'

The captain's golden hair rolled from underneath his cap. He took in the scene with piercing blue eyes. 'This here's my second-in-command, First Lieutenant William Royce.' Royce touched his cap by way of a salute.

'Well, we sure are glad to see you, Cap'n Stearne,' Dixie said.

She began to tell the story of what had happened to them and how they came to be there.

Stearne leaned forward in his saddle and listened intently.

'Our orders are to proceed to White Fir, set up camp there and make the place secure.' He gestured towards the road. 'As you can see, we are escorting the Butterfield stage up to White Fir so that anyone can have safe passage back down to Sacramento. I'm sure I can take your word that there's no one left up there. I'll have the stage driver turn round here and take you people back down.'

'Not me,' Virgil said. 'I gotta get back up to White Fir to pick up my camera.' Then he added, 'If you let me ride along with you, Captain, I could photograph you and your men taking possession of the town. That's something my editor would surely like to see.'

Stearne lightly brushed each side of his golden moustache with the back of his hand. He smiled proudly at the thought.

'You can ride up on the supply wagon, young man.'

'An' me,' Doc said. 'I gotta get back to my cabin. Paiute ain't gonna bother us no more, I reckon.'

Stearne nodded in agreement. He drew himself up to his full commanding height.

'If the rest of you would make your way over to the Butterfield, Mr Royce will order the driver to turn round. Order a detachment to accompany the Butterfield, if you would, Mr Royce.'

Filled with admiration, Dixie, Lisa May and the rest of them followed the two officers over to the waiting column of men. Frenchie helped Tom along. Black Jack hung back behind the others.

Sunlight glanced on the jingling harnesses and twinkled on the gold buttons. The soldiers sat upright in their saddles, puffing out their chests and raising their chins so that they would have to look down their noses at any enemy they might come across. The red-and-white plumes on their caps fluttered in the afternoon breeze. Their belts, bridles and the black leather peaks of their caps were polished to a shine. The green stripes down the legs of their britches were in perfect parallel, man to man. The whole band of military peacocks delighted in being looked over.

At the head of the column a young soldier carried a blue standard edged in gold braid. It carried the legend 'Sutter's Rifles – Organized June 26 1852' in red-silk letters.

'One of the best-drilled corps of fighting men in the whole country,' Stearne announced proudly, when he was close enough for the soldiers to overhear him.

16

Yellow light from the oil lamps lit the restaurant. Jingzhi set up a trestle-table for the four of them near the door and brought plates of steaming rice and fish. They sat on benches and devoured the food. Everyone was too exhausted to speak.

'They'd let us stay here,' Tom said. 'They got beds upstairs.'

Frenchie pushed his empty bowl away from him. 'Not me.' He winked at Dixie. 'I got work to do.'

Frenchie stepped over the bench and headed for the door. He paused to brush the shoulders of his jacket with his hand to try to give himself an air of respectability. He waved to them.

'You be careful now,' Dixie called after him.

'Where's he going?' Tom said.

'Oh, he'll be spendin' the night at some gamin' house, the El Dorado or one of the others. He may have rolled us up a stake by mornin'. If he don't, I'll be lookin' for a saloon to sing in for a while.'

Lisa May was falling asleep at the table.

'Come on,' Dixie said. 'Let's me an' you go an' git some

shut-eye. You ain't no use to no one if you can't stay awake.'

Jingzhi took them upstairs.

Black Jack sat at the end of the table opposite the door. Tom sat facing him.

'I know you had a gun on me, under the table, all the time we was eatin',' Black Jack said. 'You forgotten I saved your hide?'

'I ain't forgotten,' Tom said. 'I ain't forgotten you shot my brother Jeb neither.'

'I tol' you 'bout that.' Black Jack looked hard at him.

'There's a bounty on you. I should turn you in.'

'You'll have to shoot me first,' Black Jack said. 'I ain't sittin' in a cell in a militia post, while some stuffed-shirt lawyer works out what to charge me with.'

'There's somethin' else,' Tom said.

Black Jack looked at him across the table. Tom pulled back the hammer of his Colt.

'You an' your boys took our gold. I want it back.'

Black Jack laughed. 'You think I care about that now?'

'I gotta farm back in Missouri and I gotta sick pa. That gold is gonna pay off the mortgages an' the doctor's bills,' Tom went on.

'Let me tell you somethin'. I had a farm back East. It went all to hell. Three bad years an' we had more mortgages than you could count. Then my wife got took by the influenza. Weren't nothin' left for us. Me an' my boys came out West. You an' me, we ain't so different.'

'I ain't nothin' like you,' Tom said. 'Don't you never even think that.'

'All I wanna do now is to get outa here,' Black Jack continued. 'I'll work a passage down to San Francisco. Take my chances from there. I ain't planning' on stayin in California no more. Jus' put yer gun away an' let me go.'

'You gotta give me my gold back.'

'If I had it, I'd give it to ya,' Black Jack said. 'I lost it.'

'Lost it?'

Everyone in the restaurant turned to stare at them.

'Up in White Fir. At a game o' faro.'

'Frenchie's got it?'

Black Jack nodded.

'How do I know you ain't holdin' out on me?'

'Well I sure ain't got it in my pocket, if that's what you're thinkin'.' He stood up and pulled out his pants pockets.

'You coulda hidden it somewhere. Up in White Fir, maybe.'

'I ain't never goin' back up there, an' that's fer sure.' Black Jack said. 'Look, why don't you ask Dixie?'

Tom followed Black Jack up the narrow wooden stairs, holding the Colt in the small of his back.

'I thought you might get aroun' to askin' me 'bout that.' Dixie said. 'Frenchie didn't know this 'un had stole it off you when he won it. That's the truth.'

'He still got it?' Tom asked.

'He's usin' it for our seed money. That's where he's gone tonight. If the cards fall right an' if he don't get caught cheatin', he's lookin' at rollin' up a stake big enough to set up a new Bon Ton Saloon. We was plannin' on makin' you an offer, Tom. But we gotta see if he wins first.'

'It's better than havin' it stole, I guess.' He holstered his gun. 'I thought he musta hidden it somewhere.'

Black Jack was already walking down the stairs.

'Hey,' Tom yelled.

Black Jack kept walking.

'I said, hey.'

Tom ran down, grabbed Black Jack by the shoulder and spun him round.

'Whatcha gonna do, shoot me? I ain't lettin' ya turn me in.' Black Jack looked into Tom's eyes and laughed. 'You're right. You ain't nothin' like me. You ain't gonna shoot me. What good would it do, anyways? I ain't got yer gold no more.'

The kitchen door swung open, catching Tom on the shoulder. Jingzhi stood there balancing a tray full of bowls of rice. Momentarily distracted, Tom stepped aside to let the door open. It was enough for Black Jack. He knocked Tom's gun towards the wall and shoved Tom back into Jingzhi. The tray upended and bowls of rice and fish went everywhere. Jingzhi yelped with surprise. Black Jack flung open the door and dashed into the street. Tom fired. The bullet bit into the woodwork.

Tom picked himself up. He hauled Jingzhi to her feet. Jingzhi, with rice in her hair and surrounded by broken crockery, exploded with a stream of vehement Chinese. Tom made for the street.

Outside, the Chinatown crowds heaved and jostled as usual. People headed for the food halls and the gambling joints. Tom caught sight of Black Jack down at the corner, shoving his way through the crowd. Tom holstered his gun and went after him. It was no use. The street was jammed. Black Jack had too much of a start. Tom decided to head for the waterfront. He would catch up with him there.

Front Street Quay was almost deserted. The outgoing tide made rivulets and eddies on the surface of the water.

Boats strained at their moorings. As usual, groups of men were sitting beneath the plane trees. It was a cloudy night and the moon was covered.

Tom walked the length of the quay peering into boatyards, freight yards and around the piles of crates, coils of rope and timber-stacks. He reached the far end and turned to search again. There was a shout from one of the men under the trees and sounds of confusion further down where the boats were moored. The fishing dinghy Tom had noticed before was drifting downriver through the darkness. Someone was leaning over the stern, paddling with their hands.

Night was heavy over the water. Tom couldn't recognize the man from here, but he knew it must be Black Jack. He drew his pistol and fired. The shots echoed like thunderclaps across the river. The boat drifted on into the darkness.

The owner of the dinghy ran up to Tom.

'D'ya get 'im? That's my boat.'

Tom peered after the dinghy. It was too dark to see.

'Reckon I mighta,' Tom said.

'I can't go fishin' tomorra without my boat,' the man said. 'You didn't shoot the boat up none, didya?'

The dinghy was buried in the darkness down river.

Knowing he had to forget Black Jack for now, Tom holstered his gun and headed back into town to the gaming houses. The Eldorado was a two-storey wood building with a heavy oak door. Two Chinese doormen stood outside on the porch. When it was clear to them that Tom hadn't got any money, they refused to let him in. It was the same at the other gaming houses. No one stopped him entering the gambling joints in Chinatown, though, and he stood in the smoky rooms watching dice games for a while. He couldn't find Frenchie.

Back at the restaurant, Moshushi pulled out the old straw mattress that Tom had used before. Tom laid it down at the foot of the stairs, inside the front door and lay down, determined to stay awake until Frenchie returned. Within minutes he was asleep.

Pale light was filtering in through the windows when Tom woke. His body was stiff and cold. The place was full of damp river air. He got to his feet to try to warm himself up. He could hear a clatter of pans as Jingzhi started her day's work in the kitchen. Either Frenchie had stepped over him, while he slept, or he had not yet returned. Jingzhi brought him a cup of green tea, set it down on the table beside him.

Tom and Lisa May helped Jingzhi cut up vegetables when Moshushi got back from the market. The morning went by slowly. By lunchtime, Frenchie still had not returned.

'Sometimes it's like this,' Dixie confided. 'The big games kin go on for days.'

Tom got fed up hanging around the restaurant. He went back to the El Dorado. The doormen were gone and the front door was locked. The other gaming houses were also closed up. He walked along Front Street, where the riverboats were docked. It was as crowded as usual. The stevedores were busy unloading flour sacks from one of the boats and stacking them straight on to a line of waiting wagons. Sam was there, with a clipboard in his hand, laughing with a group of dockers. Tom looked for Black Jack but didn't see him.

Frenchie was waiting for him back at the restaurant. His

face was ashen and there were black shadows under his eyes. But he was smiling. Dixie and Lisa May were with him.

'I bin looking for you,' Tom said.

'I heard.'

'We got somethin' we want to say to you, Tom,' Dixie said.

'I just got back from the lumber yard,' Frenchie said. 'I put in an order for enough timber for us to make a wood-built saloon, just like Dixie is always talkin' about. It's gonna be delivered up to White Fir soon as we give the word.'

'We gonna have a new piano,' Lisa May broke in. 'Not some ol' broke down joanna with half the keys missing, like what I bin used to.'

'Thing is,' Frenchie said, 'I had to use the gold I won off Cheetham as a stake. So Dixie an' me want you to be manager of the new Bon Ton, when she's open, as partners with us. You'll be able to roll up a lotta money. Gonna be the best saloon on the Sierras. Those boys up there ain't got nothin' but gold-dust, so we aim to help 'em part with some of it.'

'You ain't got the gold no more?'

'That's what I'm sayin'. I invested it. Anyways, I didn't know Cheetham had took it off you, when I took it off him.'

Tom considered. 'It's a mighty nice offer, Frenchie. I appreciate it. But I gotta think about gettin' back to Missouri. There's the farm. My pa ain't well.'

'If the army's made it safe up there, it'll take six weeks to get her built an' ready. Three months after that you'll have made your stake back an' more. I know I reckoned it right.'

Lisa May looked at him. 'I never played a new piana before.'

'It's a good offer, Tom,' Dixie said. 'You kin sell your claim, or keep her on top o' that.'

'I gotta think, 'Tom said. 'I'm gonna take a walk down to the post office. See if there's any mail for White Fir. I ain't heard from home in a long time.'

The street was packed. Men edged through the crowd, pushing barrowloads of vegetables to the restaurants. Fishermen hauled handcarts displaying their morning catch. Conversations broke into arguments on the street corners. A newspaper-seller shouted the headlines, a sheaf of the day's papers over his arm. A couple of girls appeared at the window of the cat house opposite, laughing and calling out to guys in the street.

Tom pushed past everyone, missing home.

The post office clerk shuffled through a wooden box marked 'White Fir', peered at the envelopes and eventually handed one over.

'Tom and Jeb Hope, right? This'un came last week. Took a while to get here. Mail from Missouri ain't bin gettin' through on accounta the Injun attacks.'

Tom's heart leapt in his chest. Ruth had written. He sat down on the boardwalk outside the post office door and read. The letter was dated nearly four months previously. The noise and hustle of the crowd fell silent for him as he heard Ruth speaking. She chided him for not writing more. The weather was warmer now. The pear trees, the apples and the walnuts were just coming in to blossom. The farm was looking better than it had for a while, even though the barn needed repairing after the storms in January and there were shingles off the house roof again.

The dogs were driving everybody mad as usual and one of the bitches had slung a new litter. They were hoping for a good summer.

Then the tone of Ruth's letter changed. There was something she had to say and she wished Tom and Jeb were there so she didn't have to write it in a letter. The bank had foreclosed on the farm. She and Pa had till the end of the month to get out. The same had happened to a neighbour further upriver. Pa Hope had been to see the manager, but it was out of his hands. The bank's head office back East had ordered the foreclosure of all mortgages in arrears on farms under a certain acreage and the quick sale of the properties. They already had purchasers lined up. Plantation owners from Texas were waiting to buy up land along the Missouri River where prices were cheaper.

Pa Hope was not well. The worry of all this had weakened him. With the farm gone, they had no choice but to come out to California to join Tom and Jeb. The family would make a new life there. Pa and Ruth had arranged to join a wagon train which would be leaving in ten days' time. The journey was 2,000 miles and would take six months. Ruth would act as cook on the journey, to pay for Pa to ride on the wagon. Tom reread the letter twice. Allowing for the time it had taken for the mail to reach Sacramento, it meant they were already over halfway there.

Pacing up and down Front Street, Tom hardly noticed the crowds and the shouts of the longshoremen. His head was filled with images of home. Pa on the porch, leaning on the rail, gazing out over the back yard. The apple orchard. The apricot trees. The dogs playing in the long grass in the field beside the river.

Frenchie had said it would take three months minimum to roll up his stake at the saloon. It was already too late to save the farm.

Tom walked slowly back to the restaurant, Ruth's letter still in his hand. He hadn't told them about Jeb. He would have to hope that Pa was strong enough to take the terrible news when they arrived. All he could do was to fix up somewhere for them to stay.

Back in the restaurant kitchen, Lisa May was helping Jinghzi gut fish. Dixie was talking to the girls in the cathouse across the street, trying to recruit dancers. Frenchie was asleep upstairs.

17

Bon Ton Saloon, White Fir. Two Months Later.

Dixie had been rehearsing the girls in a dance routine all morning. A polished-walnut piano with brass candleholders shaped like growing vines stood beside the stage. Lisa May sat on the piano stool with a cotton rag in hand, polishing the brass. At a signal from Dixie, she would put the rag down and launch into a heroic, swirling tune. In response, the girls wheeled and turned across the stage, taking tiny steps and making grand, flowing gestures with their arms, right down to the tips of their fingers. They arched their necks backwards and turned their faces to smile at an imaginary audience. Every few minutes Dixie clapped her hands, bringing everything to a halt to draw the girls' attention to some fault with the steps or the smiles or the arm movements. While she explained to them, Lisa May began polishing again.

Frenchie sat at a green-baize table in the corner rehearsing shuffles. He was a master of them all: overhand, underhand, riffle, hindu, weave and strip. He practised dealing fast. He slid cards alternately off the top and the bottom of the pack and slung them to where the players would be sitting. Then, with a single, fluid movement, he swept up the semicircle of cards and began again, opening with a different shuffle every time.

Tom was standing behind an oak-topped bar. He had just finished polishing rows of tumblers and lining them up on the shelf behind him.

'Stage should be in soon,' he called out to Dixie. 'I'm gonna wait for her over by the Pony Express office.'

Tom was dying to see Ruth and his pa just as much as he was dreading giving them the news about Jeb. Dixie waved to him in reply and went back to her rehearsal.

A few minutes later, Doc burst in.

'Not yet Doc,' Dixie called. 'We ain't open till tonight.'

'I know, I know. You gotta take a look at this.' He threw down on the bar a copy of the *California Daily Star* folded open at the centre page. 'Stage just brought the newspapers up from Sacramento.'

In the bottom corner was a small advertisement. Doc read aloud: 'Samuel J. Brannan, proprietor of Brannan's Pharmacy and General Goods, Front Street, Sacramento takes pleasure in informing all his customers that a new product, namely *Doc Morgan's Cure-All*, will be in stock shortly. The 'Cure-All' is a concoction of delicately balanced remedies drawn from ancient Paiute herbal cures.' Doc looked up proudly.

'See that? That's my name, right there.'

Dixie, Frenchie and the girls had joined him at the bar.

'That ain't all,' Doc said. He cleared his throat and checked to make sure they were all paying attention. He continued reading. 'What The Cure-All does for humanity. Briefly, Doc Morgan's Cure-All almost instantly stops all pains and aches, headaches, neuralgia, rheumatism and even toothache. It settles a nervous stomach, cures gripes, catarrah, sleeplessness and other everyday ills.'

'Ain't there nothin' it don't cure?' Frenchie said.

'Tom's the livin' proof,' Doc explained. 'It's what I gived him. You only gotta look at 'im. Chipper as a jaybird, ain't he?'

'I thought you gived him whiskey,' Frenchie said.

'Nope,' Doc said. 'Whiskey was for me.'

'Well, that's mighty impressive, Doc,' Dixie said.

Frenchie refolded the newspaper, back to the front page.

'Hey. You never tol' us 'bout this, Doc.'

'Oh yeah, I was comin' on to that.'

The headline read A FORTUNATE ESCAPE AT WHITE FIR. Underneath it was a engraving of a surprised-looking Paiute brave peering round a door.

'That fella Virgil, he's done told the whole story.'

Frenchie followed the closely typed words with his finger.

'About us hidin' in the Pony Express office, about Tom comin' an' about that bounty hunter. Says Black Jack Cheetham, last of the notorious Cheetham gang, disappeared an' is suspected of bein' at large in the California gold-fields. Well, that ain't right. Last Tom saw of 'im, he was driftin' down river to San Francisco.'

'Let me see,' Dixie snatched the paper almost before Frenchie had finished reading.

She read the story aloud. Then she said, 'Says "by Virgil B. Flute, Goldfields Correspondent, Artist and Photographer".'

'Does that mean he's gonna come by here again?' Lisa

May asked.

'Maybe it does,' Dixie said. 'There's more on the inside pages. Says: "The picture on the front is a copy of the photograph taken by Mr Flute, which is the first ever taken of a Paiute Indian, and is on display at the *California Daily Star* office, First Street, Sacramento". Then there's more about Captain Stearne an' the Sutter's Rifles makin' White Fir safe.'

'Them pretty boys didn't make White Fir safe,' Doc snorted. 'The Paiute done that. They're the ones stopped the young bucks from bein' out on the shoot. Cavalry arrived when it was all over.'

'Well,' Dixie said, 'that Captain Stearne sure cuts a swell, so far as I'm concerned.' The dancers laughed.

'He's comin' to the openin' tonight with his fellow officers, so he told me. So you girls better quit gigglin' an' git the tarantella right, that's all I kin say.'

'Read out the newspaper story again, Dix,' Frenchie said.

'Once more, then,' Dixie said.

'And the part inside, about the army.'

They sat down round the table and Dixie started to read.

The door opened suddenly. A young soldier stood there. A ginger tom cat was in his arms. The girls were all smiles.

'Cap'n Stearne presents his compliments, ma'am. He sent me roun' to enquire about the arrangements for your Grand Opening tonight. Found this little fellow on guard duty outside your front door.'

Dixie jumped up and snatched the cat.

'Ted.'

She cradled the tom cat lovingly.

'Ain't seen 'im since the night we all had to hide in the Pony Express office. I thought he wasn't never comin' back,' Dixie said. 'Thank you, young man.'

The soldier nodded. 'My pleasure, ma'am.'

'We're openin' tonight at eight o' clock. You kin tell Cap'n Stearne first drink is on the house. Tom will reserve a table for his party. There'll more 'n' likely be a crowd. I hope you'll be comin' too, young man. These ladies will be looking for dancing partners later in the evenin'.'

The soldier blushed. 'I ain't one for dancin', ma'am. But I sure will be comin', soon as I get off duty.'

With the girls' eyes on him, he became suddenly awkward.

'I'll be sure an' pass on the information to Cap'n Stearne, ma'am.'

In an effort to maintain his dignity, he touched the peak of his cap and nodded to each of the girls in turn.

'Ladies.'

He stepped smartly outside. When the door closed behind him, the girls clung on to each other in fits of giggles.

Dixie looked down at the cat. 'Where have you been, you rascal?' She hugged him to her and tickled him gently under the chin. Ted stared up at her with his champagne eyes and started to purr.

'Come on, Dix,' Frenchie said. 'Read it to us.'

Dixie began again ' "A Fortunate Escape at White Fir".'

The others sat back and hung on her every word.

The door opened again. It was Tom. He ushered two other people into the saloon.

'This here's my pa an' my sister Ruth,' he said. He

beamed with pride. 'They made it all the way from Missouri.'

He introduced them to everybody by name, and Dixie, Frenchie and the girls stepped forward and shook their hands.

'Mighty nice to see you,' Dixie said. 'Any relative o' Tom's is a frien' o' ours. I know Tom's found you some rooms above the Pony Express for now, but if there's anythin' we kin help you with, you've only gotta ask.'

'That's a kind offer, ma'am. Tom only tol' us good things about y'all.' Pa Hope looked round the new-built saloon. 'Sure is a swell place you got here.'

'You come at the right time. Tonight's the grand openin'. The girls are gonna dance. A party of officers from the regiment is comin'.' She turned to Ruth. 'Kin you dance, Ruth?'

'I ain't never tried, 'cept round the kitchen at home.' Ruth blushed.

'Well,' Dixie said. 'This is California. You kin do what you want to here. If you've a mind to try dancin' you jus' let us know.'

'I kin cook good,' Ruth said. 'I could help in the kitchen, if you like.'

'We got us a fine cook,' Dixie said. 'He an' his sister came up from Sacramento with us. Nice people. Real hard workers. They could sure use some help. Tom'll introduce you. Now, I got to get back to rehearsing, if you don't min'. Come on, girls.'

Tom caught sight of the newspaper on the bar.

'Virgil wrote our story,' Dixie said. 'Show yer pa. Said that Black Jack Cheetham is still at large in the goldfields.'

'That ain't so. He tol' me he wasn't gonna stay around

in California. Saw 'im headin' downriver to San Francisco, anyhow.'

Dixie led Lisa May and the dancers up to the stage to continue running through the tarantella. Tom sat his pa down at a table near the bar and gave him the newspaper.

Behind the bar, the kitchen door was open. Through it you could see piles of plates and bowls on a long wooden table. A sack of rice was open on the floor. Crates of vegetables and a box of fish were stacked beside it. Beyond that, the back door was open and blue wood-smoke played in the air.

Outside, Moshushi was building the fire. Jingzhi sat on a log, watching him. Tom introduced Ruth.

Moshushi pressed his palms together and bowed.

'Pleased to meet you.'

'Maybe I can give you a hand later,' Ruth said. 'Looks like you're gonna be busy.'

Jingzhi smiled. 'Thank you. Very busy. Opening night. Dixie say many people gonna come. Tom has told us about you. Tom a very good man.'

'Maybe you kin show Ruth what she'll have to do,' Tom said. 'I better get back to Pa.'

In the saloon, Tom's pa was intent on the *California Daily Star*. He broke off when Tom came and sat beside him and put the newspaper down on the table.

'Sure is good to see you, Tom.'

'An' you, Pa.'

'Good to be here too. This mountain air seems to suit me. My breathin' is comin' easier than it did back home.' He leaned across the table, grasped Tom's wrist and looked him in the eye. 'Don't you go blamin' yourself for what happened to Jeb, now. Sure, it's a shock to us an' I reckon we ain't never gonna get over it. But I know what Jeb was like. He'd walk into doin' things before he'd thought about what it was he was doin'. He bin like that since he was a kid.'

'It's all right, Pa,' Tom said.

'By the way, I got somethin' for you.'

'Pa, you shouldn't have brought me nothin'.'

'No,' Pa said. 'It ain't from me. A friend o' yours gived it to me to pass on to you. Me 'n Ruth was waitin' for the Butterfield down in Sacramento an' we got talkin' to this fella. Said he'd been a farmer like me and we was swappin' farmin' stories. He was a frien'ly guy. Then he said he was comin' up to White Fir too. We explained to 'im what we were doin' an about comin' up to see you. He asked what your name was. Turns out he knows you.'

'Musta bin Sam,' Tom said. 'Works on the waterfront. Got one leg. I don't know no one else in Sacramento.'

'No.' Pa laughed. 'This fella had both his legs. Kinda tall. Big built, with a beard.'

Tom shook his head.

'Anyhow, said you knowed 'im. Said his name was Jack. Asked me to give you this.'

Pa reached inside his coat and pulled out a parcel tied up with twine.

'Then he said somethin' curious. Said you an' him was more alike than you thought. Said you both lost something and nothin' could bring it back. I asked 'im what he meant, but he just said to tell you an' you'd understan'.'

Tom struggled with the string round the package with trembling fingers. He picked open the knot with his fingernails.

'When he gived it to me,' Pa went on, 'he said there was

no need for 'im to come up to White Fir no more. He just got up an' lef' before the Butterfield come in. Didn't even say "so long".'

Tom loosened the twine and pulled off the brown paper. It was a stack of greenbacks.

Pa gasped. Tom began to count the bills.

Tom looked at his father. 'It's a thousand dollars, Pa.'

'Jeez, Tom.'

Tom picked up the brown paper and began to wrap the money again. The newspaper lay on the table. Tom's eye was caught by a headline on one of the centre pages. He pulled the paper towards him. The Sacramento branch of the California State bank had been held up by a lone gunman, the previous week. The man had worn a bandanna across his face which made him impossible to identify. He took $5,000. Shots had been fired, but no one had been hurt. The robber got clean away.

'Don't say nothin' Pa,' Tom said. He stuffed the package into his pants pocket.

Lisa May was thundering out a tune on the piano and the girls were wheeling and circling as before.

'Good,' Dixie called out. 'You got it now.'

Pa looked at Tom. 'It's all right, Pa. I'll explain later. Jus' don' mention nothin' to nobody, 'til I've had time to think.'

Pa nodded.

'I gotta get on,' Tom said. 'I gotta get this bar ready for tonight.'

Ruth appeared in the kitchen doorway. 'Jingzhi's gonna teach me to cook in the Chinese way.' She beamed. 'An' I'm gonna teach her bread an' biscuits. That is, when we got an oven.'

Dixie came over with Ted in her arms. 'Looks like we're all set fer tonight. I'm thinkin' I might do some singin' later on, if the mood takes me. What's up with you, Tom? You're lookin' mighty pleased with yourself.'

'It's a great day, ain't it Dixie?' Tom said. 'For all of us.'

Dixie looked round the saloon. Frenchie was arranging his cards in perfect piles on the green-baize table. Lisa May was giving the piano another polish. The dancers were sitting round a table with their feet up on the chairs. Pa was turning the pages of the *California Daily Star.* She tickled Ted under the chin.

'Reckon it is, Tom. Reckon it is.'